UNSCHOOLED

ALSO BY ALLAN WOODROW

Class Dismissed

The Pet War

UNSCHOOLED

ALLAN WOODROW

SCHOLASTIC INC.

Text copyright © 2017 by Allan Woodrow
Illustrations by Lissy Marlin

This book was originally published in hardcover by Scholastic Press in 2017.

All rights reserved. Published by Scholastic Inc., *Publishers since 1920*. SCHOLASTIC and associated logos are trademarks and/or registered trademarks of Scholastic Inc.

The publisher does not have any control over and does not assume any responsibility for author or third-party websites or their content.

No part of this publication may be reproduced, stored in a retrieval system, or transmitted in any form or by any means, electronic, mechanical, photocopying, recording, or otherwise, without written permission of the publisher. For information regarding permission, write to Scholastic Inc., Attention: Permissions Department, 557 Broadway, New York, NY 10012.

ISBN 978-1-338-11689-2

10 9 8 7 6   22 23 24

Printed in the U.S.A.   40
This edition first printing 2018

Book design by Yaffa Iaskoll

TO LAUREN—
YOU MAKE ME A BETTER ME . . .
BECAUSE INSTEAD OF JUST A "ME"
THERE'S A "YOU AND ME"

1
GEORGE

As we enter the school gym, the heat hits me like a steam train. I scrunch my nose to keep sweat stink from entering my nostrils. The gym is always hot, but today it feels hotter.

"Please take a seat," Mr. Foley, my teacher, instructs my class, his forehead dotted with beads of sweat. "And no running."

To my left, I see my best friend, Lilly, already sprinting past a few slower kids. I lose sight of her for a moment, but it's easy to spot her red hair and flapping ponytails.

"Lilly! Hold up!" I call out.

"You're as slow as Elvis," she teases, waiting. Elvis is her class's pet turtle, and he's so slow I bet he couldn't outrace a snail. "I am just super excited for the assembly to begin."

"As long as we're on the same team."

"Of course we'll be on the same team. Stop always being a worrywart."

"I would hate not being together . . ."

"We'll be on the same team," she insists.

We walk up the middle bleacher aisle, and Lilly sits next to Sarah and Grace. They are in Lilly's class. They both have curly hair, are dressed in identical skirts, and grumble when they need to slide over to make room for us.

"Do you think Principal Klein will announce the prize?" Lilly asks me. She wiggles on the wooden bleacher bench. She's wiry and springy and bouncy.

I blink and scratch my head. "Prize?"

Lilly looks at me like I'm an alien from another planet. "The prize! Don't tell me you forgot. The school is giving away a prize to whichever team wins Spirit Week."

I've heard about the prize, of course. Everyone has. "I think we should just play for fun," I say.

Lilly shakes her head. "Are you crazy? Playing for fun isn't fun at all."

Luke sits right above me, and he wiggles and fidgets on his seat almost as much as Lilly. "I heard the prize is ice-cream cones. All you can eat ice-cream cones forever and ever. A truck a week." Luke's leg dances up and down and his body wriggles. "Or maybe popcorn balls."

Sarah leans closer to us and shakes her head. "I heard the winning team gets to be on the front cover of *Tween Beat* magazine." She fluffs her hair. "Perfect for me."

"With a pullout poster, too," says Grace, also fluffing her hair.

"That would be awesomesauce," says Lilly, still bouncing. "But we'll hear what the prize will be soon." With her and Luke springing up and down, I'm getting seasick.

Principal Klein walks to the microphone in the center of the gym. The fifth-grade teachers stand behind him. Principal Klein clears his throat. I pull out my notebook.

"Why do you have a notebook?" asks Sarah, rolling her eyes.

"I don't think we're going to be tested on an assembly," adds Grace, also with an eye roll.

Lilly pats me on the shoulder. "George always brings a notebook." She flashes me a smile and whispers in my ear, "It's a little weird. But I like you anyway." She gives my arm a playful squeeze.

Our principal taps the microphone to make sure it's working. A big BOOM, like a thunderclap, bursts forth from the speakers and echoes through the gym.

Lilly's green eyes light up and shift back and forth, which they sometimes do when her mind is racing all over the place. "Maybe we can choose our own snacks if we win. Or maybe we'll all win jelly beans. Or phones. Or electric scooters."

"Good morning, students," says Principal Klein. A hush falls over the bleachers.

"Maybe everyone will win a puppy!" exclaims Lilly. "I've always wanted a puppy."

"I don't like puppies," says Sarah, wrinkling her nose. Grace nods in agreement.

"Please be quiet," says Principal Klein. He has a loud and commanding voice. I uncap my pen. Our principal raises his hand, motioning us to silence.

"Maybe we will win a moon rock," suggests Lilly. She is the only one speaking, but I'm not sure she notices. "I don't know what you would do with a moon rock, but that would be, like, the best prize ever."

"I need everyone quiet," says Principal Klein. He's a big man, and even though he always wears an orange cardigan sweater, he reminds me of an army general, if army generals wore orange sweaters.

The bleachers are silent. Lilly opens her mouth to speak, but then changes her mind and closes her lips. But she still bounces, and so does Luke behind me.

Principal Klein smiles and says, "I'm delighted to be here with you, fifth graders. I have some exciting news."

"I bet it's about the prize," says Lilly between bounces.

"Ssshhh," I urge with some exasperation, my finger over my mouth.

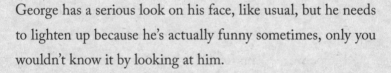

2

LILLY

George has a serious look on his face, like usual, but he needs to lighten up because he's actually funny sometimes, only you wouldn't know it by looking at him.

He furiously scribbles notes while Principal Klein speaks.

"As you know, on Monday we continue a long Liberty Falls Elementary School tradition," our principal says. "Monday marks the beginning of Spirit Week, and it's only for our fifth graders."

I let out a loud "Woo-hoo!" and a bunch of other kids yell, too. I've looked forward to this week all year, but the absolutely most amazing part of Spirit Week is Field Day. Field Day is filled with events like balloon fights and egg tosses.

Last year I snuck out of class to watch Field Day. My teacher yelled at me for sneaking out of class, and so did my parents, and so did Principal Klein.

But it was worth every yell. Field Day was awesomesauce.

"Spirit Week is about fair play," continues our principal. "It's about teamwork and friendship. It's a reward for your hard work the last five years. A celebration of sorts before you go on to Liberty Falls Middle School."

A whole bunch of cheers erupt around us. I can't wait until we start middle school next year, and I turn to George, but he's still taking notes, so I turn to high-five Sarah instead. She looks at my palm, shrugs, and then slaps my hand.

"Each of you will be assigned to participate on one of two teams," says our principal. "Team Red or Team Blue."

"I hope we're Team Red," I whisper to George. Red is my favorite color, and not just because my hair is red. Well, maybe because my hair is red, but I'm glad my hair is red, because some people have boring-colored hair and that wouldn't suit me at all.

George finally looks up from his notebook. "As long as we're on the same team, I don't care what color I am." His teacher is Mr. Foley and mine is Mrs. Crawford. Every year their classes are on the same team.

This school year is the first time George and I have not had the same teacher. Last summer, when I found out we were going to be in different classes, I was so mad I almost made a giant sign that read UNFAIR CLASS ASSIGNMENTS!

I was going to march in front of the school with it, but Mom wouldn't let me.

I was also going to make a giant frown-y face out of clay. I'm pretty good at making things out of clay. It calms me. I can also hold my breath for forty-two seconds, which is a pretty long time.

But it's been a long year without George sitting next to me in class. At least we'll be together during Spirit Week.

Principal Klein continues. "As most of you know, each team wins points based on a different contest every day, culminating with Friday's Field Day. Field Day is worth half your team's points. In the past, we've played just for fun. But we're doing something new this year. At the end of the week, the team with the most points will win a special prize."

Almost everyone in the bleachers starts talking at once. I begin bouncing in my seat again because sometimes my legs just have to bounce. Behind me, Luke says, "I bet everyone wins an ant farm."

"A kitten!" shouts Jessie, who sits in front of me. "Wouldn't that just be incredible if everyone won a kitten?"

"No," says Sarah, while rolling her eyes. "I don't like kittens."

"Me neither," adds Grace.

Maggie, who sits in front of George, turns around and grins and straightens her glasses. "Maybe we'll win a trip to the new science center that opened up downtown."

"If the prize is a trip to the science center, I don't want to win," says Sarah.

"I don't like science centers," says Grace.

"Well, if I want to get into Harvard someday, I have to really know my science," says Maggie, ignoring Sarah and Grace's frowns. "Going to Harvard is sort of a family tradition. My great-great-great-uncle was one of the first African Americans to ever graduate from there."

Maggie is the smartest kid in our school. I bet she'd make a great teacher someday. She'd probably make a great teacher now! She's in Mrs. Rosenbloom's class, and even though she's new, I hear she's pretty nice.

Everyone talks and argues about the mystery prize, and Principal Klein has to say "Please settle down" and raise his hands a bunch of times before we quiet.

"What's the prize?" yells someone from across the bleachers.

"It's a surprise," answers Principal Klein. "The prize will be revealed at the end of the competition."

Probably half the kids in the bleachers groan. I do.

Our principal continues. "This year, Mrs. Crawford's and Mrs. Greeley's classes will be on Team Red, while the students from Mr. Foley's and Mrs. Rosenbloom's classes will be on Team Blue."

My mouth falls open and all bouncing leaves my legs. George and I are on different teams? Every time I've ever thought about Spirit Week—and I've thought about it a zillion times—I've always pictured George and me side by side, passing eggs or tossing water balloons together.

George's smile falls, too. "It'll still be fun," he says, but he doesn't sound like he means it.

"We need a volunteer from each team to lead their team to victory," announces Principal Klein. "Who wants to lead Team Red?"

Despite my disappointment, both my hands immediately shoot up as if pulled by invisible strings. Being a team leader wasn't something I had planned, but planning is overrated. Sometimes you just have to do what you have to do, and I do want to win the mystery prize, whatever it is.

Principal Klein looks right at me. "Okay, then. The Team Red captain will be Lilly Bloch."

"Yes!" I exclaim, and George looks up quickly enough to exchange my hand slap.

I just know I'll be the most fantastic team captain ever, because I hardly ever lose at anything. I was only in Adventure Scouts for one year, but I sold more cookies than anyone, and

I've won 228 straight games of tic-tac-toe against George. That has to be some sort of world record.

My team will win by so many points that the school will probably build a statue of me, or name the gym after me, or something like that.

"Congratulations," says George.

I grin and grin and my cheeks hurt, I grin so hard. "I wonder if the team captain gets an extra prize? Like, if everyone got a puppy, maybe I'd get two puppies. Or two lifetime supplies of ice-cream cones."

"I doubt it. But being a team captain is a lot of work," George cautions, wearing his Mr. Serious look. It's a look he sometimes has when he thinks I'm not thinking, and I know he means well, but I can think perfectly well without his help. Most of the time anyway. "It takes organization to lead a team. And note taking. And arranging things."

I laugh and look at his notebook. "Maybe you should be team leader, then. You've got the note-taking thing down."

Then Principal Klein asks, "And who wants to be the Team Blue captain?"

George actually looks like he's thinking about it, but Maggie's hand quickly pops up.

"Thank you, Maggie Cranberry," says Principal Klein. "Why don't our two team captains come down and get their team leader pins?"

I jump out of my seat as if my legs are on springs. I practically leap into the aisle, ready to head down the bleachers.

I don't know what that special prize is, but I know it will be extra, extra awesomesauce and that no one is going to stop me from winning.

3
GEORGE

As Lilly leaps from her seat, I wonder if she knows what she's getting herself into. Leading a team takes a lot of responsibility and planning. Lilly's not very good at that sort of thing. She never has a number two pencil for tests, and she hardly ever brings an umbrella on rainy days. Last year she lost her math textbook twice.

But I'm excited for her as she hops into the aisle.

"We'll crush Team Blue!" Grace yells. She has this low, gravelly voice that sounds as if it should come out of a bigger person.

"Of course we will. Losing is for losers," Sarah says, and she and Grace wrap their pinkies together and exchange a firm pinkie shake.

Lilly looks back at Sarah and Grace, grinning. She isn't watching where she is going.

Maggie slips past the final person in her row, stepping into the aisle just as Lilly steps down.

Lilly's foot hits Maggie's leg. Maggie cries out and starts to fall. So does Lilly.

Lilly's arms wave as she tries to keep her balance. One of those arms smacks into Maggie's head. Lilly's other foot steps on Maggie's foot. Lilly's shoulder slams into Maggie's chest.

Both of their arms wave up and down, but unless they can flap and fly away like birds, none of that arm waving is going to do them any good. They both tumble backward. Maggie squeaks, "Help!"

Lilly screams, "Oh no!"

I yell, "Someone catch them!"

But it's too late. As Maggie topples over, her glasses fly off her face and her body teeters toward the ground. Lilly's legs twist around Maggie's legs. Maggie hits the wooden floor of the bleachers first. Lilly lands directly on top of Maggie.

Everyone gasps.

"Ow, my arm," cries Maggie.

"Ow, my everything," groans Lilly.

Lilly slowly eases herself off Maggie and stretches her arms and legs. She seems to be unhurt, but Maggie lingers on the ground, moaning.

"Sorry," says Lilly. "I'm so, so sorry," she repeats. She looks horrified as Maggie sits up, cradling her arm and yelping. The yelps remind me of a dog, like the ones I've seen in cages at the pet store hoping to be noticed and let out.

Mrs. Bigelow, our school nurse, marches up the stairs with a determined look of purpose. She kneels down next to Maggie. The nurse gingerly touches Maggie's arm, and Maggie lets out another yowl.

"I think it's broken, dear," Mrs. Bigelow says to Maggie.

Maggie yelps even louder, over and over again. She most definitely sounds like a caged dog.

Lilly stands frozen to her spot, a look of guilt across her face.

Mrs. Bigelow helps Maggie to her feet, and they walk slowly down the aisle, picking up Maggie's glasses as they go. Tears drip down Maggie's cheeks, although her yelping has stopped. Soon, both she and our nurse are out of the gym, but everyone remains silent.

"Winning Spirit Week just got easier," says Sarah, breaking the quiet. She has a small, cruel smile on her lips.

Grace smiles, too.

Lilly still stands in the aisle. "That was an accident, I swear." She bites her lip and tugs on her ponytail.

Sarah and Grace shake their heads as if they don't quite believe her.

"I hope Maggie is okay," our principal says worriedly. He

speaks so loudly that his voice booms across the gym even without the microphone. But then he leans into the mic and his voice grows even louder. "I'm sure we will all keep Maggie in our thoughts." He looks down at his feet as if unsure what to do, but then he clears his throat and continues. "Unfortunately, we will need a new captain to step up and lead Team Blue. Does anyone else want to be Team Blue captain?"

I'm still thinking of Maggie and her yelping, and I feel terrible for her. I raise my hand.

I instantly regret raising it, but Maggie will take over as our team captain when she gets back to school, hopefully on Monday. As Lilly said, I'm good at taking notes. I can fill Maggie in on everything as soon as she's recovered.

"George Martinez. Terrific," says Principal Klein. "Why don't you and Lilly head down the bleachers?" He pauses and then adds, "And, please, please be careful."

I exit the aisle. Lilly waits patiently and even lends me her arm so I don't stumble getting out of my row. She squeezes my arm as she leans into my ear and whispers, "It looks like we're enemies now." She says this with a smile, so it's a joke, I think.

"Yep, that's us—enemies forever." I laugh as we step down the aisle together. "Just remember: Winning is about organization and planning."

Lilly laughs. "It's called Spirit Week, not Organizing and Boring Week. And no one can out-spirit me."

A few kids cheer as we step onto the gym floor and approach Principal Klein. I'm not sure if they cheer because we are captains, or because we walked down the bleachers without falling. I hate standing here, with everyone's eyes on me, but I focus on our principal and try to ignore the bleachers. He holds two shiny badges. They look sort of like police badges, except made of cheap bronze-colored plastic.

"These were the only pins they had at the store," Principal Klein mumbles to us as an apology of sorts. My team leader pin features a picture of a goldfish with the words I LOVE GOLDFISH! underneath it.

"Congratulations, George," says Mr. Foley.

I throw him a smile and a thumbs-up. "I'm sure it'll be fun."

"That's the spirit!" says Mr. Foley.

After we pin our badges to our chests, Principal Klein steps up to the microphone again. "Spirit Week begins on Monday with our first official contest: Twin Day. Everyone should pick a teammate and dress in identical clothing. The team with the most and best matches will get five points. I'll personally judge Twin Day on Monday morning right here in the gym." He clears his throat, smiles at Lilly and me, and adds, "Just remember, the week is about spirit and teamwork. Let's compete with good sportsmanship. I'm sure you'll make Liberty Falls Elementary proud."

Nearly every kid in the bleachers applauds, but I notice Sarah and Grace do not. They whisper to each other, quietly huddling, as if they are passing secrets.

"Good luck," I say to Lilly.

She grins back to me. "You bet."

But I notice that she doesn't wish me good luck back.

As we join the rest of our grade in exiting the gym, Lilly hurries ahead of me and reaches Sarah and Grace. The three of them walk off with their arms around one another's shoulders, and I get an uneasy feeling about them.

I don't want to compete against Lilly and secretive Sarah and Grace. I regret volunteering to be team captain even more.

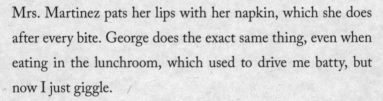

4
LILLY

Mrs. Martinez pats her lips with her napkin, which she does after every bite. George does the exact same thing, even when eating in the lunchroom, which used to drive me batty, but now I just giggle.

We have dinner with the Martinez family every Friday and sometimes we eat at my house and sometimes we eat at George's house and sometimes we meet at a restaurant. Restaurant nights are my favorite Friday night dinners, especially if they let George and me pick where we go, because George always lets me pick.

But tonight dinner is at my house, and I hate that because Mom makes me clean up my stuff first, and it's not easy picking up an entire week's worth of clothes and junk from every room. I usually cram everything into my closet.

We host more dinners than the Martinezes host dinners,

and I'm pretty sure it's because Mom likes me cleaning up stuff. Thankfully, she never looks in my closet.

"I hear you are both Spirit Week captains," George's dad says. Mr. Martinez always wears a tie because he works in an office, unlike my dad who works out of our house. George looks a lot like his dad. They both have the same dark eyebrows and tan skin and they both look serious all the time. I think George will wear a tie every day when he's older.

"Hard to believe." George beams. "I didn't really want to be captain. But someone needed to step up, at least until Maggie is back."

"We're proud of you," says his mom. "It's not easy being a team captain, even for only a day or two. It's a lot of responsibility."

"And we're proud of you, Lilly," says my mom. When I got home from school and told her the news, she gushed and hugged me and acted like it was a really big deal.

She flashes me a smaller smile now. Mom isn't the sort to fuss over me in front of other people.

To George I say, "You guys don't have a chance."

"We'll see," says George in his serious tone. "It's all about organization, you know."

I shake my head. "It's all about winning."

"Well, I hope it's a tie," interrupts Mr. Martinez.

"Amen to that," says my dad. "I'm sure you'll both be great leaders, and you'll have a lot of fun no matter who wins."

"Just remember you two are best friends," adds my mom.

Moms say the weirdest things sometimes. "Why would we forget that?" I ask.

"Competition can bring out the ugliness in people," says Mr. Martinez, frowning.

All the parents nod their heads, and my mom looks right at me. She keeps her stare fixed on me.

"What now?" I ask.

"Remember Adventure Scouts a few years ago, and your cookie sales?" Mom takes a bite of her lasagna, but she continues to watch me.

"Sure, I sold more cookies . . ."

"You stole Francine Pepper's list of cookie sales," says Mom. "That's how you sold so many cookies."

"I didn't steal it!" I insist. "She gave it to me."

"Because you promised you'd be her best friend."

"I was her best friend for a whole week, so I kept my promise," I retort with a frown. So I like to win? Who doesn't? "I even earned enough points for a free sleeping bag."

"I just know how you can be sometimes," Mom says.

"It would take a lot more than Spirit Week to break this

team." I motion to George and me. "Team George and Lilly is way more important than Team Red or Team Blue."

"I'm glad to hear that," says Dad.

"Just remember that friendship is forever and the silly Spirit Week is only a week," adds Mom.

"It's not silly," I say. "There's a giant prize this year for the winning team, and it's probably better than an Adventure Scouts sleeping bag. Principal Klein won't say what the prize is, but I hear it's something like a trip to Hawaii. And don't you want me to win a trip to Hawaii?"

Dad laughs. "I don't think the school could afford to send half the grade to Hawaii."

"Well, I'm sure it will still be a great prize," I say. I wish Spirit Week started right then. I'd prove to everyone that my team is unbeatable and show my parents what a fantastic prize we all get. "My team is going to win, and win big." I glare at George.

"Stop it, Lilly," says Mom.

I break my stare and remind myself that the week is just for fun. I laugh at myself. Maybe I can be a little competitive, but like Sarah said, losing is for losers. I dig into my lasagna again. Mom still watches me as if she's worried I'm going to do something terrible, but a little competition won't get in the way of my friendship with George. We've been best friends since before I can remember anything. My parents even have pictures of us sleeping next to each other as babies.

In each photo, I'm lying in the middle with all the stuffed animals while George is curled off to the side. If we ever fought over the stuffed animals, then I won every time.

5
GEORGE

Lilly's bedspread is a confusing maze of pink diamonds and green swirls. Her walls are bright blue and her carpet is orange. I always get a headache if I stare at the carpet too long. But I can't see that much of it anyway, because her floor is usually covered with clothes and books and random things like a stuffed bear and a shoebox. I grit my teeth as I look at everything that's out of place. I want to walk around and clean it all up.

This is why I never spend much time in Lilly's bedroom. I always feel like screaming at the mess. Once I made the mistake of opening her closet. It's all empty hangers and balled-up clothes on the floor. I offered to help her organize all her clothes, and even started to diagram a special area for sweaters, but she wasn't interested.

Her dresser and shelves are lined with small clay figurines of all sorts, including a guitar without a neck, a ballet dancer with only one leg, a soccer player with no arms, and a unicorn without legs. Lilly isn't great at finishing things, although she loves making things out of clay.

I have a miniature U.S. Capitol building in my bedroom that she made for me last year. The bottom half looks just like the real U.S. Capitol. It doesn't have a top half though, and that's sort of the most important half.

On the floor by my feet is a deck of cards. Lilly and I used to play all the time, but we played Go Fish a few weeks ago and I won by accident, because I usually let her win, and she hasn't wanted to play since.

She's not a good loser. One time she bought two Hula-Hoops, and it turned out I was really good and Lilly wasn't. She threw the Hula-Hoops away the next day.

"It's right here," Lilly says, digging through her sock drawer. "At least I think it's here." She tosses socks around the room, which just adds more mess. I wonder how she can find anything in such a disorganized disaster of a room.

"Oh, I've got them," she says at last. I think the drawer is now empty of all socks. She holds out two bracelets made of interwoven green, red, and blue string. She hands one to me. "A friendship bracelet."

"What's that?"

"We each wear one. It means we're best friends. Forever."

"I don't need a bracelet to know that." But I tie it on my wrist. Lilly does the same. I throw her a big grin. "Thanks. It's pretty great."

"Just like me," says Lilly, but with a playful smile. "Mom bought me a kit, and I started them a few weeks ago, but then I think we had dinner and I put them away and sort of forgot. But anyway, here they are." She beams.

As I look at the bracelet hugging my wrist, I forget all about Lilly's glare at dinner. I just hope Maggie is feeling better. Our parents might have been excited that we are both captains, but I'm not. I think it's more fun to take notes than to give them. I've been taking plenty of notes for Maggie. I'll pass them to her when she's back at school, hopefully on Monday.

"And don't worry about the stupid Spirit Week and us being captains," Lilly says, as if reading my mind. "It would take more than a contest to break us apart." She throws me a smile, and it's a warm smile, one that I can feel deep down in my stomach all the way up my chest and down my arm where my new bracelet is wrapped snugly. "But that doesn't mean I don't want to win."

"I think we'll give your team a run for your money," I say with a smile.

"You can try, but we're not going to lose," Lilly adds, but she is not smiling. "And I'll do anything to win." She glares at me, the same glare from dinner. But then she breaks the glare and giggles. "I'm just goofing around."

But I honestly can't tell if she's totally goofing around or not.

6

LILLY

I don't know why George feels his team has a chance to beat my team this week. He seems to think I can't even organize my lunch.

Which, by the way, I did today all by myself—a cheese sandwich and some cookies and a bag of chips. I forgot the fruit, but so what? Fruit is overrated.

On Friday, Principal Klein gave George and me a list of the events planned for the week so we could prepare, and I read it over during the weekend, or at least I read most of it because I was busy doing other stuff. Mom bought me some new clay and I made a totally incredible penguin, except I didn't finish its beak or feet. But otherwise it looks exactly like a penguin, sort of.

Today, Monday, is Twin Day, and Team Red has this contest wrapped up like a cozy blanket. Because it turns out that

I'm an organizing queen, even if George doesn't think I am. Saturday morning I called Sarah, and she was going to text Grace, who was going to text a few other people, and then Aisha volunteered to call a few kids from class, and so I'm sure someone reminded everyone, somehow.

There is no way Team Blue can match our matches.

Aisha and I are twins today. It wasn't easy figuring out what clothes made sense, since she wears sweat pants and team jerseys almost every day and I don't play sports like she does. But we both have red sweaters, so we wore those and that's perfect because we're Team Red. I own two of the same scarves, because I thought I lost mine last year but I found it under my bed after Mom had already bought me a new one, so we're wearing those, too. Aisha also bought two silly straw hats at the party store yesterday.

I haven't seen Aisha yet this morning, but she came over to my house last night and we swapped clothes. We will look fantastic together.

It feels a little weird being Aisha's twin, since I always thought George and I would be twins today. He has these goofy orange beanies, and I figured we could wear those, and we were going to buy matching shirts, but you can't be twins with some-one from the other team, obviously.

Mom dropped me off early at school today. Every Monday morning I eat breakfast at school because she has to leave early for work, and George comes early, too, because his mom and my mom work together. As soon as I enter the cafeteria, I look for George.

I can't wait to see his face when he realizes Twin Day is Team Red day, but I don't feel quite as confident after I look around.

It's like I'm seeing double, and not just Team Red double, because every fifth grader I see has a twin. Two lunch ladies are dressed alike, too. They wear pirate hats and eye patches.

My stomach sinks. I should have known Team Blue would be ready. If I'm an organizing queen, George is like the note-taking and organizing king of the universe.

Noah says the special prize is a road trip to the Grand Canyon. Aisha says that's not true, that the winning team gets to go to a soccer game, or a baseball game, or a track meet, or some sort of sporting event but she can't remember what.

Either way, we would miss school, so we have to win. If we go to the Grand Canyon, I'll spend my entire time writing postcards to George, bragging about how great our team was and that I'm having the best time ever.

Well, maybe that would be a little mean. I'll end every postcard with a big *I miss you!* and a smiley face because I would miss having my best friend with me.

I pay for my orange juice, oatmeal, milk, and a banana. I thank the lunch lady, who says, "Arrrr you sure that's all you want?" in a pirate growl. I tell her that I'm sure, and then I look around for George.

He's sitting with Luke at a table in the middle of the room. They both wear extra-large yellow shirts with George's goofy orange beanies.

I feel a twinge of hurt. That was supposed to be me in the orange beanie and not Luke. Part of me wants to ignore George because the beanies were my idea in the first place. But I look down at my wrist and see my friendship bracelet. Friendship is way more important than beanies, and Team George and Lilly is more important than anything.

Of course I know that already, but the bracelet is a nice reminder.

I'll walk over to George, wish him good luck, congratulate him on his great organizing skills—and of course mention how mine are just as good—and then we'll eat breakfast together. There's no reason today shouldn't be like every other Monday. Just thinking of sitting with George makes me feel good.

Grace waves to me, walking over. She wears giant plastic glasses and a red T-shirt that says TEAM RED IS FABULICIOUS! and in smaller letters TEAM BLUE STINKS! "Sarah and I made these last night."

"Awesomesauce," I say.

She points to a table in the far corner of the lunchroom, which is where she usually eats. "Let's sit over there and have breakfast. Sarah and I were talking while we made these shirts last night. We have some ideas on how we can win."

"Like what?" I ask.

"I can't tell you here." She looks right and left, and then left and right, and then she whispers, "Someone might be listening."

"Listening to what?"

"Secrets." She fluffs her hair and smirks.

George sees me and waves, and I smile back. Grace has never asked me to eat breakfast with her before. She and Sarah usually eat by themselves, and it would be nice to eat with her and hear about her secret plans. But I guess they can wait until later. "I'm going to sit with George. I always do."

"But he's on Team Blue," Grace says with a look of horror spreading across her face.

"He's just George." I weave past a group of third graders to join my best friend. "Hey, George," I call out. "Nice out—"

I never say *fit* as in *outfit*, which is what I wanted to say. George stands up as I approach him, and I guess I'm not expecting him to stand up, so I stutter-step, and I don't know where that leg came from, but my foot hits someone's leg.

My lunch tray flies up. I reach for it, but instead I knock the tray and make it flip completely over.

I see the tray turn and spin and flip like it's in slow motion, but like a slow-motion horror movie.

My orange juice soars into the air as if spouting from a water fountain. My oatmeal forms a gray, flying, lumpy cloud. My milk spins from its cup like a sort of mini-tornado.

I can see where everything is going to land before it does.

Everything is going to land on George.

SPLAT!

The oatmeal bowl ends up oatmeal-side down, right on George's head, on top of his orange beanie.

SPLASH!

The juice completely drenches his shirt.

SPLOOSH!

The milk sprays his shoulders.

Oatmeal skids down his face and liquid drips from his shirt.

"Oh no!" I say. The entire cafeteria stares at us in silence. I know how George hates messes, and he's just a giant mess. He stands there, in shock. "I'm so sorry!"

Then I hear someone clap and Grace call out, "That's the way to do it, Lilly!"

7
GEORGE

"Now where is that box? Oh, there it is." After a moment of thinking, Mrs. Frank, our school secretary, drags a large cardboard box from the corner of the walk-in storage closet. The shelves of the room are filled with envelopes and pencils and binders and lots and lots of paper. I've never seen so much paper. Mrs. Frank breathes heavily as she pulls the box to the middle of the floor. Her gray-hair bun sways back and forth. "Take what you need. You can change in the bathroom."

My shirt and pants stick to me with wet, cold orange juice. Big clods of half-dried oatmeal fall in flakes from my head to the floor. I smell like someone's stale and rotten breakfast. My orange beanie is ruined, too.

I washed some of the mess off in the bathroom, but a lot of Lilly's breakfast still clings to me. The small bottle of hand sanitizer I keep in my pocket wasn't helpful, either. You can't hand-sanitize your clothes and your hair and your entire body.

Mrs. Frank called my mom, but she's at work and can't get away yet. So I'm forced to change into clothes from the dreaded Lost and Found box.

I sift through clothing that has probably been here for decades. The box is filled with single sneakers, unmatched and random socks, an assortment of old jeans, a purple bathing suit, seven flannel shirts, and lots and lots of winter hats and mittens.

There is one boot, three pairs of underwear, and a belt. Who loses underwear? The even bigger question: Who loses their pants?

I picture someone walking home without pants. I hope it wasn't cold that day. I shiver thinking about it, although the cold orange juice in my underwear isn't keeping me warm, either.

The only shirt that sort of fits me is a green T-shirt that reads PANDA-MONIUM! It has a picture of a smiling panda bear on it. Most of the pants are too small. I guess younger kids lose more clothes. The only pants that fit me are a pair of old jeans with big rainbow patches on the pockets and glitter down the legs. I think about keeping the pants I'm currently wearing, even though they are messy and wet.

In the end, dry clothes with rainbow patches and glitter win. But I wouldn't be surprised if the person who wore these pants lost them on purpose.

I stuff my wet clothes into a garbage bag to bring home later and then exit the bathroom.

Luke looks bummed out when he sees me walk out into the hall. He taps his feet and wiggles his body like usual. It's like he's always listening to music in his head. But there is no happiness in his wiggles today.

"Sorry," I say. "This stinks."

"If there is another panda shirt in the Lost and Found box, I can wear the other one. We can still match." We spent half the morning on Saturday finding just the right shirts.

"No such luck."

"Great!" he replies. I throw him a frown. "I mean, it's not great that we don't match, and I have nothing against pandas, but that shirt . . ." Then he adds in a quiet, apologetic tone, "But on you it looks good." He looks me up and down. "And I sort of like the pants."

I frown. "They have rainbow patches and glitter on them."

"I like rainbows." I'm not sure if he's kidding or not.

"Let's just get to the gym," I say with a grumble. "I hope I haven't let Maggie down. But at least she can take over as team captain." I've had enough of leading a team. Being drenched in breakfast is about all I can handle.

"Didn't you hear? Maggie broke her arm in two places. She might be out all week." Suddenly, my borrowed clothes feel ten times heavier. "You're our team captain for keeps."

I groan. I don't think today could get worse. School hasn't even started yet, and not only am I wearing the world's most embarrassing clothes, but I have to march into the gym wearing them as our team captain.

I knew I never should have raised my hand in the auditorium. I could make a list of everything I know about leading a team, but I can't think of anything to put on it.

I'm glad we don't see anyone as we walk down the hall and toward the gym. I glance at my reflection in the glass trophy case that hangs on the wall.

I still have some oatmeal crusties clinging to my hair. I swat them off.

We turn the corner and the gymnasium is straight ahead. A few kids laugh when they see me. I want to hide. Hiding would really be the best thing to do, but I'm team captain now and I need to stay and support us. Team captains don't hide.

Brian and Seth stand against the wall. They are both in Mrs. Rosenbloom's class, which means they are on my team. When they see me, Seth giggles. "Nice pants."

Brian doesn't laugh. He sneers. He looks angry. Brian and Seth are the two biggest kids in our school. They are the meanest kids, too.

They are dressed in shoulder pads, football pants, and jerseys with the name of our local sports team: the Fighting Bells. They are football twins.

"We heard what Lilly did," growls Brian.

"I can't believe she would sink so low," agrees Seth, no longer giggling at my pants. His angry frown now matches Brian's. Seth makes a fist and pounds it against his open palm. "We need to teach her a lesson."

"It was just an accident," I say.

"That's not what I heard," replies Brian.

"Team Red is planning all sorts of stuff," says Seth, frowning. He bares his teeth, which reminds me of an angry bear.

He and Brian are two guys you don't want to mess with. Even Luke has stopped his usual wiggling and toe-tapping, and instead slowly walks away, keeping his distance from them.

"Uh, what sort of stuff do they have planned?" I ask, slowly inching away, too.

"Stuff," says Brian. "I don't know what, but we can't let them get away with this."

There is no way Lilly would deliberately spill her breakfast on me to win Twin Day, and I doubt she would be planning something. But didn't Lilly tell me she'd do anything to win?

Lilly then said she was only kidding, but maybe she was kidding when she said she was kidding. And didn't I hear Grace clap after I was drenched?

I look down at my wrist and at the friendship bracelet that avoided the milk and orange juice spill. Best friends forever. That's what Lilly said the bracelet meant.

"We're going to get even," says Brian, frowning.

"Team Red will be sorry they messed with Team Blue," adds Seth.

I open my mouth to argue, but as Brian and Seth glare down at me, I remember that they are kids you don't want to argue against. So I just smile and nod. "Whatever you say, guys." But I'm team captain, so I add, quieter, "As long as we play fair, right?"

"If they cheat, we'll cheat," says Brian.

Seth nods. "That seems pretty fair to me. I hear everyone on the winning team gets a free bike."

"I need a new bike," says Brian, sneering with a steely, hard look.

"Bikes are nice," I agree. The two of them are whispering to each other, I can't hear what, but they are probably planning horrible things. I should say something to them. I should argue that we need to exhibit good sportsmanship. Instead, I just repeat, "Bikes are nice."

Brian ignores my comment. "Do you like slime?"

"I guess," I say, confused. "Slime is nice, and so are bikes." I don't know what I'm saying. Just talking to Brian and Seth makes me nervous.

"My older brother can make slime," Brian says.

"Good for him," I say, grinning awkwardly.

Then the school bell rings.

"Come on," says Luke. "We have to get inside the gym for the Twin Day judging. Everyone else is already sitting." As he nudges me forward he asks me, "What were those guys saying, anyway?"

"Nothing important." I follow Luke into the gym. Meanwhile, Brian and Seth's quiet but disturbing chuckles continue ringing in my ears. I look back at them, and I know I should tell them to forget whatever they are thinking of doing, but all I say is, "Bikes are really nice, aren't they?"

"I guess," agrees Luke.

I hate myself for not saying anything more. I should make a list of everything Brian and Seth could do with slime. But I don't think I want to know what they plan to do. Some lists are better left unwritten.

8

LILLY

The gym bleachers are split in half, with my team on the side closest to the front doors. That's the better side, because sometimes you can feel a slight breeze from the hallway, but not always and not today. It's as hot as ever in here.

I look for George, but I don't see him. He ran out of the cafeteria all covered in food. Poor George. I hope he's not mad at me.

Aisha is my twin, and I have to say, we look pretty great. Sarah sits on the other side of me, and her face is one giant grin. "Nicely done, Captain."

"Great job," adds Grace, nodding. Both she and Sarah fluff their hair, although I think their hair already looks pretty fluffy.

"Thanks," I say with pride. "We got the word out, didn't we? I think everyone on our team is dressed as someone's twin today."

"Sure, that too, I guess," Sarah says with a shrug.

I look at her, confused.

From the bleacher row above me, Amelia pats my back. She removes her glasses and winks. "Nice going."

"Anything to win, right?" says Grace.

"Sure, but I don't know what you guys are talking about." I cross my arms and try to ignore them.

But suddenly I know exactly what she's talking about and why everyone is congratulating me, and it has nothing to do with my planning talents. I overhear Ruby, sitting in front of me, telling Koko that Grace told her I spilled my breakfast on George on purpose.

I want to stand up to tell her and everyone that George is my best friend and I would never, ever, ever spill my breakfast on him on purpose and I told him I was sorry.

But am I the really, truly, sorry-to-my-toes kind of sorry?

Because part of me is a little glad about it. I want to win, and if accidents happen, then that is one fantastic accident for Team Red.

Principal Klein walks up and down the aisles holding a clipboard and a marker, counting twins. He looks right at me and at Aisha, and writes a big check mark.

A peal of laughter rings out from the bleachers that are closest to the front doors. George and Luke walk in, and everyone around me bursts into giggles, especially Sarah, but

I'm not sure if I should laugh or cry. George wears glittery jeans with rainbow patches on them and a weird panda shirt. Sarah elbows me in the ribs. "Best captain ever."

I don't say anything, but a big guilty ball forms in my stomach.

George refuses to look at anyone as he trudges past our side of the bleachers, his head down and his shoulders slumped. Team Red's laughter continues, louder.

Finally, George reaches the far end of the bleachers, where he sits with his team and stares at his feet.

But while my entire team laughs, I don't hear any laughter from the members of Team Blue. They throw us dirty, hostile looks. Meanwhile, Principal Klein is checking Team Blue for twins. He writes: check, check, check, check . . . He sees George and makes a mark on his clipboard that is definitely not a check, but an *X*.

Amelia pats me on the back again. "I hear the winning team gets a free milkshake machine. Wouldn't that be great?"

"Um, no," says Sarah. She glances at Amelia and shakes her head. "I don't like milkshakes."

"Me neither," agrees Grace, and Amelia's face turns red and she doesn't say anything else. "But I like smoothies. Maybe they'll give out smoothie machines."

Sarah nods. "That's a much better prize. But whatever it is, we can't lose. Not with Lilly as our captain." Sarah and

Grace exchange pinkie shakes and then flash me wide, toothy grins.

Aisha, my twin, looks at me with her eyes wide and asks, "Did you really spill your food—"

"Of course not," I insist before she even finishes her sentence. "It was an accident."

"Good," says Aisha. "Because I'd hate to win by cheating." I feel a little better knowing that at least one person believes I'm telling the truth, but I don't feel a whole lot better, because I peek another look at sad, frowning George.

Our principal finishes his count, walks down the bleachers, and makes his way toward the middle of the gym. The other fifth-grade teachers wait for him.

Principal Klein clears his throat, stares at his clipboard, and then looks up and speaks into the microphone.

"Congratulations to both teams," he announces. "I am greatly impressed by the school spirit shown here today. I have never seen so many twins. In fact, one team has everyone dressed as a twin today! That's simply incredible. Five points to Team Red."

Everyone around me jumps up and hoots. It feels good to win. No, it feels *great* to win, and I can't keep myself from bouncing up and down. But then I glance at the end of the bleachers, where George hangs his head in his ridiculous rainbow-patched pants and panda outfit. I whoop, "We won!"

but winning just doesn't feel as great as it should, and I stop bouncing.

Winning should always feel good. We're one step closer to free smoothie machines, or whatever super surprise Principal Klein will spring on us.

But.

Part of my joy floats away like a helium balloon and circles my best friend who sits alone, dejected. I've never felt bad about winning before. It's a strange feeling. I sit down while the rest of my team continues to celebrate. Meanwhile, I can feel stares from Team Blue aimed at me. They all think I'm a cheat.

Sarah leans close and whispers into my ear as if we're exchanging a big secret. "So what are you planning tomorrow? Maybe our entire team can spill food on Team Blue?"

"It was an accident," I insist.

Sarah rolls her eyes. "Fine. Don't tell me. It's probably best to keep it quiet, anyway. You never know who might blab."

She and Grace grin.

At the end of the bleachers, George no longer looks at his feet. Instead, he looks up directly at me, and his mouth is curled into an angry sneer, just like the rest of his team. Luke says something to George, and then they both glare at me.

"High five!" cries Sarah, holding her palm out for me.

I ignore it.

Mom sits on a folding chair against the wall, waiting for me at the school office with a new, clean set of clothes. I know she hates being called away from work. She frowns with an impatient fidget as I enter through the doors.

I'm sorry that she had to come to school. But I feel worse looking in the office mirror at my outfit.

When Mom sees me her expression changes from annoyance to horror. "Oh no. What did they do to you?"

"It's just clothes, Mom," I say, grabbing the plastic bag from her outstretched hand.

"But you're a glittery rainbow panda." Then she adds, "Maybe I should take a picture to show Dad?" She hunts in her handbag for her cell phone.

"Please don't," I say. "I would rather forget I ever wore this."

Mom stops her handbag poking. She puts her arm around me as if to give me a hug, but I step back. Parent hugs are fine at home but sort of weird in public, especially at school, even if it's just in front of the office staff. "Mrs. Frank told me you picked the outfit out yourself?"

"I didn't have a lot to choose from," I say. "I guess people don't lose good clothes. I think most Lost and Found clothes stay lost for a reason." I look in the plastic bag Mom handed me. Inside are stuffed normal blue jeans and a plain striped shirt. I can't wait to get them on.

Mom kisses me on the forehead, and I let her. A kiss is faster than a hug. "Well, I hope you have a better rest of your day. I suppose it's been a difficult morning."

"It can't get worse. Unless Lilly decides to ruin something else of mine."

"It was just an accident," says Mom with a warm smile. "You know that Lilly's always been a little clumsy."

Last month Lilly helped clear the dishes after dinner at my house and tripped. A spaghetti-sauce stain still splotches the ceiling of our kitchen. "I don't know, Mom. She says she'll do anything to win. And everyone says she did it on purpose."

"You can't believe that. She's your best friend."

"I don't know what to believe."

"Well, I believe in Lilly. And you should, too."

She's right, though. I shouldn't be thinking the thoughts I'm thinking. I feel awful for thinking badly of Lilly. It makes me feel dirty, and I suddenly have an urge to spurt more hand sanitizer on my palms.

A few minutes later, after I've thanked Mom and I'm in the bathroom changing out of the panda shirt and borrowed jeans, I make a decision. Next time I see Lilly, I will apologize for even imagining mean things about her.

Everyone else might think Lilly intentionally spoiled my outfit, but I know better.

Dressed in normal clothes, with the Lost and Found outfit folded neatly and put back into its cardboard box, I feel like a new person. I hurry down the hallway to the cafeteria. I've already missed the start of the fifth-grade lunch period, so I'll need to eat quickly.

I hate eating quickly. I think the ideal number of bites is fourteen for every mouthful, and you can't chew your food fourteen times, every time, if you are in a rush.

I once experimented with twelve bites for every mouthful, and it just wasn't the same.

As soon as I walk through the glass cafeteria doors, I look for my best friend. We always sit together at lunch, and I need to show her that I don't blame her for being clumsy.

But when I see her, I don't approach her.

She sits with Grace and Sarah in the far corner. Lilly never ate with them before, but now it seems like the three of them are always together. It's almost like she has two new best friends.

Lilly laughs and Sarah laughs, and maybe it's my imagination, but they seem to laugh a little too loudly, and they look like they are plotting.

I stare at them. Lilly must sense my stare, because it's easy to sense stares like that. She looks up and sees me. She smiles, but I don't smile back. I'll just stand right here, in the middle of the lunchroom, until she gets up and apologizes.

Then, maybe, we'll pretend the accident never happened, and we can have lunch together like usual.

The sooner I forget about my rainbow pants and panda shirt, the better, anyway.

Lilly starts to rise from her seat. She's about halfway up when Sarah tugs on Lilly's arm. I can't hear what Sarah says, but Lilly sits back down. I don't move, waiting. But Lilly isn't coming. She's not even looking at me anymore. She and Grace and Sarah huddle, talking. It's pretty obvious no apology is coming.

"Over here," says Luke. He waves me to his table, where he sits with Toby and a few other Team Blue kids. I sneak one last glance at Lilly, but she's forgotten me. So I join Luke and the others from my team.

Luke scoots over to make room for me on the lunch table bench. He wiggles as always, and it makes the entire table shake a little.

"Sorry about losing Twin Day," I say.

"It's not your fault," says Toby. Toby is one of the nicest kids in the fifth grade. He's always smiling—and he's got such a big smile that you can't help but smile back. Today he frowns. It's a very large frown. "We have to get even," says Toby, frowning even deeper.

"What do you mean?" I ask.

"You know. Stand up for ourselves, do something back," Toby insists. "An eye for an eye. They did something horrible to us, so we should do something horrible to them."

"If it was done on purpose, then sure," I say. "But accidents happen."

"I hear Brian and Seth like slime," says Bjorn, who is an exchange student from Sweden and has the blondest hair I've ever seen. He looks down at his phone and starts punching buttons. You're not supposed to bring phones to school, but every time I see Bjorn, he's on one or on a computer in class or the library.

"What about slime?" I ask. I think back to my conversation in the hall with Brian and Seth that morning. I get a little worried.

But Bjorn is back playing on his phone and doesn't hear me.

"What did you hear about slime?" I repeat, but Bjorn is in his own world. Someone told me he has four computers at home.

The bell rings, signaling the end of lunchtime. I haven't even started my sandwich yet, let alone had time for my fourteen chews a bite. The rest of the group stands up to leave, and I stuff a cookie into my mouth, but it's too large of a piece and I choke.

I need to know what Brian and Seth have planned, but I'm choking so I can't say a word. Everyone walks away as I spit half of the cookie into a napkin.

I take a deep breath before I stand to go. Maybe I'm worried for no reason. What's the worst thing that can happen with slime?

But Lilly spilled her breakfast on me, possibly on purpose to win Twin Day, so even if the worst thing that can happen does happen, then maybe Team Red has it coming to them. It's not like I can do anything to stop their plan from happening, anyway. I'm only team captain because Maggie broke her arm. I'm not a leader.

As everyone walks down the hall, I stop in the bathroom to wash my hands like I always do after lunch. I wonder, if I just stayed in the bathroom all day, would someone else be named team captain? Probably not, unfortunately.

10
LILLY

Everyone leaves the cafeteria to head to class, but I stay behind because I want to say something to George. My best friend! But before I can get his attention, he walks away, surrounded by members of Team Blue, who I think all hate me.

So I wait until he's completely out of the cafeteria before I leave.

At least he's no longer wearing that silly outfit. A lot of kids in our grade dressed funny for Twin Day, including me, but his outfit was the worst, and it didn't even match a twin, and that made it even worse than worst, and it was my fault. I should have apologized to him when he walked into the lunchroom, but he looked so angry, and Sarah convinced me to stay put.

He's the enemy now, and Sarah says you don't apologize to the enemy. But George and I could never be enemies in a million, billion years. Not real enemies at least, just sort of pretend ones.

As my teammates pass me, a few say "Congrats" or throw me a thumbs-up. I flash them smiles, but behind those smiles, I feel guilty because maybe I did spill my breakfast on George on purpose just like everyone says. I mean, I didn't, but deep down maybe I wanted to spill on him. Which makes me feel terrible.

That's called the subconscious, which is what makes you do or say things you don't want to do or say but you really do deep down, and then they sort of bubble up when you don't want them to.

I trudge out of the cafeteria, and the hallways are emptying as fifth graders rush to class. I pass Principal Klein and Mrs. Rosenbloom, who both stare at a glass display case filled with trophies. Kyle Anderson won a regional poetry competition last month and his trophy is inside. Our school also won some spelling bees and a robotics fair a few years ago.

I think our trophy case should be more full of stuff. They should give Team Red a trophy after we win Spirit Week and put that in the case. I can even make the trophy out of clay for them. That would be awesomesauce.

Principal Klein's loud voice is sort of hard to miss as I walk by. "Do you know I have never won a trophy?" he says to Mrs. Rosenbloom.

"No! You must have won at least one," she says.

Principal Klein shakes his head. "Sadly, no. Not even as a child. Times have changed, haven't they? Every child wins a trophy now just for participating, but back in my day they were harder to come by. It's a regret."

"You've accomplished a lot. You're principal of an entire school."

"True. But they don't make trophies for that."

"Well, they should," says Mrs. Rosenbloom, patting him on the back.

Their voices trail off as I hurry past them, but even before I push through the large swinging glass doors that separate the fifth-grade hall from the rest of the school, I hear moaning and angry shouts.

I walk into our hall and enter a scene of total horror.

Every kid stands in front of his or her locker, grimacing and wincing. Puddles of green slime surround their feet.

My locker is near the front of the hallway. I step over a puddle of murky slime and turn my locker combination. Right. Left. Right. I open my locker.

Greenish blobby liquid pours out and onto my tennis shoes.

Inside my locker is a whole bunch of green goop. My backpack is unzipped and sitting on the bottom, and I can see that it is filled with slime.

The inside of my locker door is covered with the stuff. It appears that someone poured the slime through the open grates near the top of the door, and also hit every single locker in our hallway.

Tara, whose locker is only five down from mine, cries out: "My report on cumulus clouds! Ruined! Destroyed!"

"Who did this?" demands Finn, who is the biggest kid in my class. He's probably half a foot taller than me, and I'm not short. He slams his locker in anger. He has a wide nose that reminds me of a slightly squished potato. His potato nose twitches.

We're all wondering the exact same thing: Who would pour slime into every fifth-grade locker? And why?

But then I realize that someone didn't pour slime into *every* fifth-grade locker, because the lockers at one end of the hall haven't been slimed at all.

Those are the lockers near Mrs. Rosenbloom's and Mr. Foley's classes. Those are the Team Blue lockers.

A few of the Team Blue kids wander to our side of the hallway. Some gasp, covering their mouths. Most look as horrified as I feel. But not everyone on Team Blue gasps and groans and looks wide-eyed at the catastrophe all around my feet.

Brian and Seth, two bullies I've never liked very much, stand at the end of the hallway, laughing.

"They ruined my cat posters!" howls Jessie. Jessie always talks about her cats.

"I just earned my blue belt in karate, but now it's a green belt," wails Jai, holding up a white karate outfit tinged with green splotches.

George pushes through the doors into our hall. I don't know where he's been, but he takes one look at the horror show that is our hallway and his mouth drops open.

But I'm not buying his act. This is a Team Blue act of sabotage, and he's the Team Blue captain, so there is no way he didn't know about this plan. I slam my locker and stride toward him. "You think this is funny?" I demand.

"Why . . . what . . . when . . ." His eyes roam the hallway, back and forth, in a look of total shock. "Who did this?"

But my eyes just narrow, and I poke him in the shoulder as hard as I can. "As if you don't know who slimed us."

"Hey!" He steps back and rubs his shoulder, but his eyes remain gazing on the puddles of green muck and the shocked faces of my teammates. "Someone did this to every locker?"

"No," I hiss. "Just every Team Red locker." I can feel the anger building inside me. "If you want to play dirty, we can play dirty," I warn.

Finn marches toward us. His face is bright red. Sarah and Grace approach, too, their faces twisted in rage.

Other kids are approaching us as well. Sarah stomps closer. Grace looks furious. Even Aisha, who is normally so calm, looks like she wants to scream.

"B-But I didn't . . ." George sees everyone approaching, the same as I do. He doesn't finish the sentence. He sprints down the hallway toward the safety of the Team Blue locker side.

When he reaches the end of the hallway, a few members of his team let out a loud, "Hooray, George!"

I hear it, and so do Sarah and Grace and Finn and the rest of my team.

While Team Blue clasps George on the shoulder, welcoming their hero, I look into the angry eyes of my team members.

"If they want war, we'll give them one," says Sarah.

"We need to do something," agrees Grace. "Something terrible."

I feel a shiver up my back. "The best revenge will be winning Spirit Week, and winning the prize."

"I hear the prize is a free helicopter ride," says Finn.

"I don't like helicopters," says Sarah.

"Me neither," says Grace.

Finn frowns. "I don't like them, either, I guess."

"Whatever it is, I want to win it," says Sarah. "And if winning Spirit Week is the best revenge, then I know just the way to do it. You guys with me?"

"I am," I say, and I wrap my pinkie around Sarah's and Grace's. We all squeeze.

11

GEORGE

I hope today is a better day than yesterday, because yesterday was the worst day of my life. I don't know why I raised my hand to be team captain in the first place.

I wish I could take it back, but you can't take back things like that.

When I volunteered I never thought I would have to hide in my classroom until school was over. But that's exactly what I did yesterday. Everyone on Team Red looked so angry in the hallway, glaring at me and thinking all sorts of terrible thoughts. I know they blame me for locker sliming, even though I didn't do a thing.

Mr. Foley was nice to let me linger in the classroom after the bell rang. I told him I wanted to finish some schoolwork.

I didn't walk home with Lilly, which was strange. We always walk home together.

I hate being team captain.

I haven't even talked to Lilly since she yelled at me in the hallway yesterday. I still can't believe that she thought I had anything to do with the locker incident. How could she imagine I had something to do with that awful prank?

I push open the doors to the fifth-grade hallway and am surrounded by red shirts. At the end of the hallway, everyone wears blue shirts.

Last night I texted half my team to remind them of Color Wars Day, and instructed each person to call another person. I created a spreadsheet on my mom's computer to make sure not one kid was forgotten. I even brought two blue shirts to school today, just in case someone forgot to wear one.

I might hate being team captain, but I still have to try my hardest to be a good one.

I don't think I needed to do so much planning, though. All the breakfast spilling and locker sliming seems to have made everyone determined to win. No one wants to be the team member that costs us victory.

The hallway floor is still slightly stained with green. It might be that way for a while. Lilly stands by her locker, her bright red shirt almost matching her bright red hair. I smile and raise my hand to greet her, and even start walking toward her until I remember that we aren't speaking.

I suppose when you do something every day, like talk to your best friend, it's hard to remember not to do it. I lower my hand, turn my smile to a frown, and veer away at the last moment. She sees me though. I grunt at her. It's not a friendly grunt but just a grunt. She grunts back and then takes a step away from her locker and trips. Her shoelaces are untied.

Lilly sprawls forward, her arms waving like she's doing the dog paddle before regaining her balance. As my mom said, Lilly's always been a bit clumsy. Is she clumsy enough to spill her breakfast on me, or clumsy like a fox, using her clumsiness to get away with ruining my Twin Day clothes on purpose?

I guess I can't be completely sure of anything, except it figures Lilly would walk around with her shoelaces untied.

I always double knot my shoelaces so they can't come untied. I have a list of things I need to do in the morning, like floss. Double knotting my shoelaces is the eighth thing on my list.

I hurry down the hall to my locker. I don't feel safe surrounded by so many red shirts, and feel relieved when I blend in with a sea of blue. The exchange student, Bjorn, looks up from his phone and smiles at me. "Nice job yesterday. Or as we say in Sweden, *Snyggt gjort.*"

"But I really didn't do anything . . ."

Before I can get more words out, Adam, who is in Mrs. Rosenbloom's class, steps between us. He hands me a small yellow lollipop. "I stole this from the office," he says. "Well, not stole. They are free. I was going to give it to Lizzie, but I forgot she doesn't like lemon."

"Um, thanks," I say, accepting his gift.

Kyle, who is also in Mrs. Rosenbloom's class, slaps me on the back. Kyle is a big guy, so his slap sort of hurts and takes away my breath for a moment. His hair is almost as red as Lilly's and he's almost as big as Brian and Seth. He smiles, and when he speaks it's in sort of a half rap: "Great thinking, pouring that sticky slime. But make it extra goopy next time."

A bunch of other kids slap me on the back or just shout stuff like, "You're the man, George!"

Luke rushes over when he sees me. "Did you really do that? I mean, those guys on Team Red were so mad." He jumps up and down with excitement, like he's on a pogo stick or has springs in his shoes.

"I had nothing to do with that," I insist.

"Everyone says you did."

"I didn't."

"Well, okay. That's good, then. It was sort of a rotten thing to do, I guess. As long as you didn't do it." But he says it in a sort of *I don't believe you* way, before dancing off to his locker.

I want to shout at the top of my lungs after him: "It wasn't me! I didn't do a thing! It was Brian and Seth!"

But I don't say that. Because I see Brian and Seth huddled by Seth's locker, laughing. Brian looks at me and puts his finger to his lips, like we plotted the sliming together and it's our secret to keep.

I know what I should do. I should run to Principal Klein and explain what happened. It's my responsibility as team captain to keep my team under control.

Did I mention that I hate being team captain?

But Brian is big, and Seth is big, and I'm not so big, and I guess I don't have any proof they did anything. You sort of need proof to accuse people of really bad things like locker sliming.

A lump forms in my throat, and my feet feel cemented to the ground. Brian and Seth walk by me and I say, "I like bikes." I don't know why I say that, but I just do, with a goofy smile on my face that I wish I could erase.

Maybe I'll talk to them later about things.

As they brush by me and I simply stand there without moving, Samantha slinks up to me. She wears a royal-blue cashmere sweater with matching blue shoes and a blue headband. They are all the exact same shade. She flips her blond hair over her shoulder. "That sliming was pure genius," she says. "Let me know if you need any help with anything. I'd be happy to give you some free fashion advice sometime. You just have to ask." She looks at me, starting at my feet and going up to my head. "Like, you could use new shoes and a different haircut." She leans over closely. "I hear the special prize for winning Spirit Week is matching handbags for everyone. Wouldn't that be the best?"

I don't know what I would do with a matching handbag.

Before I can say anything about it, Samantha has already turned away to go to class.

My thoughts are interrupted by the squawk of the PA system. Principal Klein's voice is always loud, but over the loudspeaker it sounds like the voice of doom soaring through the school corridors. "This is Principal Klein. Will George Martinez report to my office? Immediately."

I hope he just wants a meeting with the Team Blue captain to congratulate me for my wonderful organizing talents. Maybe he wants to see my Color Wars spreadsheet. Or maybe he will declare yesterday a tie, because he knows Lilly spilled her breakfast on me, on purpose.

But he sounds angry, even over the PA, and my heart quickly sinks as I plod down the hall toward the office.

My teammates watch me, shaking their heads. "Go, Team Blue!" shouts Toby in encouragement, raising his fist in some sort of military salute.

A few people clap. "Stay strong, George!" Luke calls.

But as I walk past the Team Red lockers, the Team Blue claps are replaced by icy Team Red stares. This is how criminals must feel when they march into court, or maybe to jail. Every step takes me closer to the judge. It's a long walk.

As I exit the fifth-grade hall, a group of second graders point at me, whispering to one another. Even they think I'm guilty. Word spreads fast.

When I arrive at the school office, I'm relieved a police officer isn't standing there, waiting to arrest me. Mrs. Frank frowns at me from behind the front desk. She lowers her eyeglasses and shakes her head. Without a word she merely points to Principal Klein's door, which is slightly ajar behind her. I nod, approach the door, and knock before stepping inside. Only bad kids are sent to the principal's office, so does this mean I'm one of the bad kids?

The office is smaller than I thought it would be. I've always imagined a lush, giant room with expensive paintings and fancy statues. But the room is cramped, and our principal sits on a large leather chair behind a wooden desk that takes up half the floor space. He clears his throat, clasps his hands atop his desk, and nods toward the chair facing his desk. "Sit." I do.

We lock eyes, and it takes all my willpower to stay seated rather than run away in terror. He has a mess of pens on his desk, and in the silence I pick some up and put them inside a jar that holds even more pens.

"Don't touch the pens," orders Principal Klein.

"Sorry," I mumble. "They were, um, messy."

"That's not the mess you need to clean up." His eyes peer into mine as he drums his fingers on his desk.

"My room at home is clean," I mutter. "So I don't have a mess to clean up, at home I mean." I smile, as if I made a joke, but this isn't the kind of situation where a joke is appropriate, and it wasn't even really a joke, so I just bite my lip and say nothing else.

"Do you think putting slime into lockers is funny?" He asks this in a tone that implies he definitely does not think that is funny.

"No, sir," I answer. It feels appropriate to call him sir rather than Principal Klein.

"Do you think it's okay to destroy homework and lunches and other things that people keep in their lockers . . ." He pauses and I wait for him to continue. "Like jars."

"What kind of jars?" I ask. I wonder if I'm strange for not having any jars in my locker.

"Well, okay, not jars," says Principal Klein, coughing. "Never mind that. But the homework and lunches, those are in lockers." Principal Klein stares at me, his face a stone of sternness. "Fortunately, the slime washed off most of the clothing and backpacks. But some personal property was still ruined."

"It's awful, sir."

"Beyond awful. I wonder what sort of student would do something so horrible."

I sit up straight. "I had nothing to do with it, sir. I promise you."

He raises an eyebrow. "Didn't you?"

"No, sir. Absolutely not, sir."

"Because it seems odd that only Team Red lockers were slimed. It appears someone on Team Blue did this."

"I guess it would seem that way."

"And you're the team captain."

"Well, only because Maggie broke her arm. I mean, I was just the second team captain, not the first one, right? So it doesn't count as much?"

Our principal frowns. "It still counts."

I look down at my team captain badge, pinned to my chest. Even though it reads I LOVE GOLDFISH!, it represents a lot more than fish. It represents fair play and leadership. It means I made a commitment. "I know it does, sir. You're right, of course, sir," I say, keeping my head bowed. "And I'm sickened by what was done. Really."

"I see." I look up to see him staring at me, deeply staring, as if trying to peer into my brain and pluck the truth from inside my head. He sniffs, as if he's smelled innocence. "But you know who did it?"

I do, at least I'm almost positive I do, but almost positive isn't the same as completely positive. And even if I were completely positive, I know I wouldn't say anything. You don't rat on teammates who can beat you up with one hand tied behind their backs. So I shake my head. "No, sir. I have no idea, sir."

I immediately feel guilty for saying that, but then I think of Brian and Seth and their hugeness.

Principal Klein removes the pens from his pen cup, the ones I placed inside, and lays them on the table, so they are messy again. It seems to make him happy. I really, really want to stuff them back in the cup. I sit on my hands to keep them from cleaning. "Spirit Week is not about slime. Or even about competition."

"It's not about competition, sir?" I ask, blinking.

"Well, a little about competition, yes," he admits. He stands up and begins to pace. There are only a few feet of space behind his desk, so he can only take one or two steps before turning around and taking two more steps. I get a little dizzy watching him. "Competition, sure. But it's called Spirit Week because it's about spirit. Teamwork. About banding together for a common goal."

"Then why do you have two teams compete against each other?" I ask. "If it's not about competition, I mean."

"Because games bring out the spirit in you!" exclaims Principal Klein, stopping his pacing and jutting his fist in the air. He points at me. "I don't want any more hijinks, you understand me? Even if it wasn't you, it was someone on your team. This week is about fun. Have fun, and make sure the rest of your team has fun. Got it?" But there is no fun in Principal Klein's voice.

"We will have fun, sir. Good fun," I squeak.

"If there are any further problems, there will be consequences. Severe consequences. For your team and for you."

"Yes, sir. Thank you, sir. I won't let you down, sir."

"Then we'll see you and your team out on the field after lunchtime for Color Wars."

"Thank you, sir."

As I excuse myself from his office, my hands shake. Because I know he is right. Spirit Week is about fun competition, not mean-spirited competition. I need to keep my team in line. It's my job. I'm our team captain, even if I wish I weren't, and I have my goldfish-lover badge to prove it.

Sure, Lilly might be up to some tricks. I wouldn't put it past her to be planning something with Sarah and Grace right now. But the only way to show her, and everyone, that clean competition is the best competition is by winning Spirit Week. And Team Blue is going to win, and win fairly.

At least I hope everyone on my team plays fairly, because I just don't know if they will, and I really don't know how I can stop it.

12
LILLY

When you're the leader of a team you need to get everyone motivated. Last night I was going to make small clay frogs for all of Team Red. There's an animal called the red poison dart frog that's bright red and poisonous. I thought it could be our mascot, which would be awesomesauce.

But by the time I finished my research, it was sort of late and it would take a long time to make that many frogs and I only had so much clay, so I only made three of them, and I never got around to giving them legs or painting them red, so I left them at home. Maybe I'll finish them tonight. I asked Mom to buy a lot more clay, just in case.

But we don't really need motivation to win, anyway. Not today. Sarah had a great idea that should guarantee us another victory.

It's after lunch, and both teams stand outside in the large field behind the school. Hardly anyone ever comes out here, although there's a whole crew who waters and mows it at least once a week. That seems like a waste of time, just like cleaning my room is a waste of time, since it's just going to be dirty again, probably within minutes. But the field is great for Spirit Week. White lines have been laid down with chalk on the grass, forming a large rectangular court. There are two sides, separated by a line in the middle. My team is on one side, and Team Blue is on the other.

A large bucket of balloons sits near our back line. Our balloons are red and filled with chocolate pudding, and another bucket of balloons lies on the opposite side of the field. Those blue balloons are supposed to be filled with vanilla pudding.

Everyone wears a garbage bag, with holes for our head and arms. Still, this will get wonderfully messy. I know how George hates to get messy, and I feel bad for him, but then I remember the sliming and I don't feel so bad for him anymore. I remind myself that losing is for losers.

On the opposite side of the field, behind Team Blue's back line, Principal Klein stands with Ms. Bryce. They both wear garbage bags, too. Ms. Bryce used to teach fifth grade, but that's a whole other story.

She and our principal will decide who wins today's event by determining which team is least covered with pudding, so if there is more chocolate pudding splattered, we win.

There is no way we're going to lose.

But this day is going to be fantastic for another reason, too. I love pudding! If a few pudding drops fly into my mouth, it will be like an extra bonus treat. I start to bounce on my toes just thinking of winning and eating pudding.

Aisha approaches me. "What's the plan, Captain?"

I blink and stop my toe bouncing. "The plan?"

"Right," says Aisha. "The strategy. How are we going to beat them? Do we all throw balloons at the same time? Do we scatter? Do we form a giant wall?"

"Don't worry," I assure her. "Just throw your balloons as fast as you can. I can guarantee you we're going to win."

Aisha frowns. "What do you mean?"

"Trust me."

I look at the other side of the field, where George stands with his team. He walks up and down, arranging kids this way and that way. Knowing George, he probably spent hours mapping out a strategy for today. That would be just like him.

Well, it was a waste of time.

"I'm ready," says Finn, his mouth frowning with grim determination. "They slimed us yesterday, and we're going to pudding them today."

"We're going to *extra* pudding them," says Pete. He looks like a shorter version of Finn. They both wear angry scowls.

"I'll be like a cat. Fierce and quick and mean," says Jessie. "Well, not mean. Cuddly. Cats are cuddly. But I'll be quick and catlike."

Many of my teammates stand near us now, watching me. I guess they expect me to announce some big strategy.

I do have a strategy. Revenge. "We've got this won, easy. No worries."

"It's fabulicious," Sarah agrees, and holds out her pinkie for me to shake it. I do.

Sarah and Grace say playing fair is for losers. That's true. If I had played fair and hadn't been Francine Pepper's best friend for a week, I would never have won a free Adventure Scouts sleeping bag.

Mom says I should feel bad about winning that sleeping bag, but it was really Francine's fault for giving me all her cookie sales so she could be my best friend. Well, that and maybe because I told her that if she was my best friend, I would let her ride my pet unicorn.

My entire team is listening. George might have better organizing talents than me, but being a team captain is about a lot more than organizing. "Guys, just go out there and throw those balloons as hard and straight as you can. I promise that at the end of the day, we'll show those Team Blue slimers they can't mess with Team Red. We will win. We will be victorious." I smile because *victorious* is a pretty great word to use. "We are Team Red!"

Everyone starts shouting, "We are Team Red! We are Team Red!" I join the cry. "We are Team Red!"

Tara lets loose a howl.

But Aisha lingers a second and glares at me. I ignore it. Glares don't win free trips to the moon, or whatever prize we're winning. I just hope we don't win Adventure Scouts sleeping bags. Mine broke the first time I used it, so it wasn't even worth all that fuss with Francine Pepper.

As we break up the huddle to grab our balloons, my stomach feels a little queasy. Because as much as I want to win and as much as I want to hate George and blame him for the sliming incident, I know deep down, as far deep as anything can go, that George didn't do anything. Not him.

On the other side of the field, Team Blue is ready. George stands stiffly in the very back corner of his square. He has no idea what's about to happen.

My team shouts, "We are Team Red!"

I echo their shout, but not as loudly as I should. "We are Team Red."

Sarah and Grace laugh.

I just wish I didn't feel so guilty for what's about to happen.

13
GEORGE

Each member of our team holds a balloon. So does every member of Team Red. I studied battle formations from great wars in history, and I think I have my team ready. Those who can throw farthest are in the back, like archers. My fastest members are up front, where they can dodge and dart.

Team Red kids just stand around, clumped randomly. It's obvious they have no organization.

I'm happy with my strategy, and I'm even happier about what I'm wearing. I put on some old jeans and a T-shirt and a pair of swimming goggles. I don't want to ruin good clothes with pudding stains or get any food in my eyes. Even though I'm wearing a garbage bag, it won't keep all the pudding off me.

I'll need to keep my mouth closed, too. There is no way I want to get pudding in my mouth.

I brought a brand-new bottle of hand sanitizer for today.

Last year's fifth graders were covered head to toe in pudding after Color Wars. I once heard a rumor that a kid was so covered in chocolate pudding that his teammates accidentally ate him. I don't think it really happened, but you can never be too sure about that sort of thing.

While I'm dressed for pudding, not everyone is as prepared as me. Samantha stands only a few feet away in her cashmere sweater. I don't think she'll be very happy if pudding gets under her garbage bag.

"Remember," shouts Principal Klein. "No stepping out of bounds or over the midline. After all the balloons are thrown, Ms. Bryce and I will determine which team is more pudding-drenched. If we see more chocolate pudding covering fifth graders, then Team Red wins, and if there is more vanilla pudding, then Team Blue will be declared the winner. You will start and stop on her whistle. And remember, there is absolutely no throwing at anyone's head."

Brian and Seth stand next to me. They are in the back, because they can throw far, and I'm in the back so I can study the field and make last-second adjustments, and so I don't get dirty. Brian and Seth each cradle three balloons. They wear extra-wide smiles on their faces.

"Remember the plan," I instruct them. "Aim at their best throwers first. Once we hit them, the rest of the group will be easier targets."

"I'm just aiming for heads," says Brian.

"Most definitely heads," agrees Seth.

I should probably demand they drop their balloons and refuse to let them play if they don't play by the rules, but instead I just smile and nod. "Heads. Right. Great," I mumble.

Before I can say anything else stupid, Ms. Bryce blows her whistle. And the balloons fly.

Dozens of red and blue globes fill the sky. The sounds of splattering rubber surround me.

"Hey!" yells Lacey as a giant lake of chocolate pudding smothers her chest.

"Yuck!" yells Avery, another pudding victim.

A balloon lands right by my feet and another narrowly misses my face. Red balloons crash all over the field, covering the ground and my teammates, and at least one hits Principal Klein, standing behind me.

I hear him yell, "Oh no! There go my slacks."

Chocolate is everywhere. I toss my balloon, not aiming at anyone in particular and just hoping it hits something red. I don't see it land.

I had a plan, but it is obvious no one is following it. Kids in the back run to the front, and those in the front cower in the back. My teammates toss their balloons as randomly as I did. Seth and Brian seem oblivious to the destruction, hurling balloons as fast and as hard as they can, each wearing large grins.

But although we're drenched in chocolate pudding, the Team Red side is in much worse shape. I watch one of Brian's balloons as it sails toward Lilly on the other side. The balloon is on target, down, down, down. She doesn't see it, but I watch the entire arc.

It smashes into her stomach and douses her with a big stain of chocolate pudding, some flying onto her face. She smiles as she licks chocolate pudding off her lips.

Wait. She's licking chocolate pudding?

But our balloons are supposed to be filled with vanilla pudding.

That's when I realize what I should have realized immediately. Not only is my team covered with splotches of chocolate pudding. All the garbage bags worn by Team Red drip with chocolate pudding, too.

A balloon flies over my head and toward Principal Klein. He sidesteps but crashes into Ms. Bryce. The balloon explodes onto their garbage bags.

Below me, the field is a wet, sticky marsh of brown pudding. Principal Klein shouts, "Stop! Wait!" but I can barely hear him over the yells of my teammates. Seth and Brian continue to hurl balloons in groups of three or four each.

A balloon smashes into my shoulder. It stings for a split second, but then the pain is gone and all that lingers is a puddle of chocolate pudding dripping down my chest and onto the bottom of my old jeans.

"Stop!" yells Principal Klein again. "I said stop!" Ms. Bryce blows her whistle, and a few more balloons soar into the air. They fall harmlessly except for one balloon, one final heave from Seth that rises and then falls and splatters on Lilly's head.

Lilly is already so full of pudding that she looks more like a swamp pudding monster than my best friend. At least I think we're still best friends.

Ms. Bryce's whistle shrieks again. Everyone stares at her and our principal. No more balloons fly.

I can barely see the grass at my feet. It's as if we are all in some shallow chocolate-pudding lake. The ground is muddy and brown and sort of disgusting.

I want nothing more than to take a bath and change my clothes. I fish my hand sanitizer from my back pocket and give my hands a great big squirt. But I would need a few gallons of sanitizer to wash all the muck off me.

By now, I think everyone has noticed there is no vanilla pudding anywhere. I hear Luke say, "Does this mean we lose?"

I suspect sabotage.

Principal Klein and Ms. Bryce huddle together. They are close enough that I can hear their conversation. But then, Principal Klein never speaks softly. They both seem to be as confused as I am.

"I thought half the balloons were supposed to be filled with vanilla pudding," says Ms. Bryce.

"Yes, of course," agrees Principal Klein. "That was the plan. There appears to have been a mistake."

"Do you think so? I mean, technically Team Red wins. More chocolate pudding covers kids than vanilla pudding."

"Yes, I guess Team Red wins," answers Principal Klein. But then he shakes his head. "Well, no. We can hardly call it a fair victory, can we? I believe Grace and Sarah were supposed to fill the balloons. Maybe they just lost track of the pudding."

"Yes, it was an accident," agrees Ms. Bryce.

"It has to be," says our principal.

But I don't buy it. Not for a moment. Sarah and Grace are no accidents, and I wouldn't be surprised if Lilly was in on the whole thing from the start.

Our principal walks into the Color Wars court. He trudges carefully, but he's a big guy and his feet sink into the murk with every step. Pudding splashes onto his pant cuffs. His voice booms across the pudding-pond field. "It seems there has been a dreadful pudding error today. Obviously, we cannot declare a winner. We will call today a tie."

A dozen moans fly from our side, but even more moans echo from Team Red.

"That's not fair!" yells Sarah from the other side of the field. She practically growls, and both Grace and Lilly's faces appear just as angry.

Principal Klein ignores the comment. "Please file into the school where clean towels await. We will resume Spirit Week with our next contest tomorrow."

"A tie?" grumbles Brian. "We had this thing won."

"By a mile," agrees Seth.

On the other side of the field, Lilly shouts, "Since today doesn't count, does that mean Team Red is still ahead?"

Principal Klein frowns but calls back, "I suppose it does."

A few Team Red members let out a cheer, as if their cheating victory yesterday is all that matters.

I can't help but notice Lilly exchanging high fives with Sarah and Grace. I stare at Lilly's broad smile gleaming from within her chocolate-smeared head. She runs her finger across her pudding-caked cheek and then plunges her finger into her mouth.

Sarah and Grace grin madly.

"They're a bunch of cheats," says Brian. "They knew we

would win. That's why they messed around with our balloons."

"Of course they did," agrees Seth.

"We need to get revenge," says Brian. "Spread the word. Lilly's a cheater. That whole team is filled with cheaters."

I want to argue that playing fairly is the only way to play, but it's hard to think about that when it's obvious Team Red will do anything to win. So I just smile and nod and bite my lip. Team Red is filled with cheaters, and the proof is in the pudding.

Maybe I should just let Brian and Seth do what they need to do. Brian probably should have been team captain and not me.

14
LILLY

George stands at the edge of the sidewalk that leads from the entrance of our school. I think he's waiting for me, but I decide to walk past him without saying a word, because I know if I say anything, it will probably be something mean.

We've walked home together every day since first grade, not including yesterday, because I think he was hiding after the sliming-locker trouble.

I haven't said a word to him all day today, and I've never gone a whole day without speaking to George, at least none that I can remember, except when I went off to camp, and even then I wrote to him.

Still, I march past him. Maybe I feel a little guilty for agreeing to the pudding plot. I didn't actually fill the puddings, but I knew about it and I agreed to it. I know losing is for losers and everything, like Sarah says, but maybe winning is not only for winners, not always.

"Nice way to cheat today," says George.

I can feel my face go red. I turn to him, and I can't keep the words in my mouth. I know they are mean, and I know they are unfair, but I think it's my subconscious acting up again, or my guilt, or both.

"Only one team can lose, and it won't be us," I reply. George opens his mouth to say something back, but I don't let him. "And you're the one who poured slime into our lockers. You told everyone I spilled food on you on purpose. So don't you dare say anything about our pudding."

George holds his hands up as if he's surrendering, while stepping back. "I didn't do any of that. I didn't slime. And I didn't tell anyone you spilled food on me on purpose."

"You are such a liar!" I exclaim.

George stops retreating and stands up straight. Now he's the one who looks angry. "I am not a liar!" he shouts back at me. I don't think I've ever seen George yell. He looks sort of mean when he raises his voice. "You're the one that ruined my Twin Day outfit. You started everything."

"And I'm glad I did!"

"So you admit it? You admit you ruined my outfit on purpose?"

"I don't admit anything except knowing your team deserves whatever is coming to it."

I'm not sure I believe what I'm saying. I don't really want

to say any of these things, and I feel guilty for cheating, but I'm so worked up I can't stop what I'm saying from flying out of my mouth. It feels good to see George shocked. If we're going to have an argument, then I want to win it.

"It stinks you were slimed, but at least we haven't cheated," says George. "You need to start playing fairly or . . ."

I cut him off. "Or what? We both know what you and your team did. And we both know what you're doing and what you're thinking of doing, and none of it's any good, and you pretending you're not doing anything just makes it all worse."

"You're the one who says you'll do anything to win."

"At least I'm not the one crying about fair play." I continue to stare and fume. I think about the mystery prize for the week, which may mean being mayor for the day, or we get to be in a movie, or something else just as great, and I want to win whatever it is more than anything. "I don't even know why we were friends to begin with."

George's face falls. He takes a small step back. "You don't know why we're friends?" he asks, sputtering. "But—we've been best friends forever."

"Maybe I don't need a best friend anymore."

I hate those words. I don't feel them, and it's as if someone else is saying them, and it's someone I don't like, and it's the same person who agreed that all the balloons should be filled with chocolate pudding today.

But the words come from me, even if they don't feel like they are, and even if I can't stop them from reaching George's ears.

"Fine, maybe you're right," he grumbles.

I want to take back what I said, but I want even more for him to take back what he said. Only it's too late, and now he's puffed out his chest and mine is puffed out and we're staring at each other, our faces only inches apart.

I could hug him. I could put my arms around him and apologize. That's all it would take, really. A hug and an *I'm sorry*.

But I don't do any of that, because all I can hear are the words *losing is for losers* over and over again in my head.

George rips something off his wrist. It's the friendship bracelet I gave him. He holds it in his left hand, the threads torn, the strands waving in the wind. "I guess I don't need this anymore, then." He throws the bracelet to the ground.

A gust of wind blows the ripped bracelet into a bush next to us, wrapping around small brown thorns, half hidden in the greenery. I look up at George.

This whole argument is my fault. I have said too much. I'm clumsy and I ruined his outfit and never apologized, and then it's all gone downhill from there. But I can't even see straight, because my eyes are watery and my anger is steaming and my guilt is swimming and, well, I feel about a million different things tugging me this way and that way.

So I turn away, not saying a thing, leaving George behind me, and I walk home alone for the second straight day.

George doesn't follow me.

I grip the friendship bracelet I'm wearing on my wrist and try to rip it off like George did, but I can't. Mine is knotted tighter and the anger has seeped from my body. I barely have the strength to walk. I untie the bracelet strands, which isn't easy to do while walking, and it takes the better part of two blocks to untangle the knot, and by then I'm already near the street that leads to my neighborhood. I chuck my bracelet into a sewer grate on the side of the curb.

My wrist feels bare, but maybe it's for the best. I told George I didn't need a best friend.

I hope I was right.

15
GEORGE

I get home and hand Mom a note from Principal Klein. It tells her how I was called into his office today and that lockers were slimed and balloons were messed up and as team captain I'm expected to set an example. It doesn't actually accuse me of anything, though.

I've never brought home a note from school before. My hand sort of trembles when I give it to Mom.

She reads it and looks at me and reads it again and looks at me again. "Did you have anything to do with this?" she asks me.

I shake my head. "No."

"Did you know about it?"

I'm about to say I didn't, but I also know that's not entirely the truth. I knew something was going to happen, I just didn't know what. I know who probably did the sliming and pretended I didn't know. But I can't lie to Mom, because I've never lied to her, just like I've never lied to Lilly, although maybe I sort of did today.

Is silence the same as telling a lie?

"I *think* I know who did some of that." I look down at my feet. "But." Mom raises her eyebrows. "But they're really big kids," I blurt out.

"So?" asks Mom, and it's obvious she doesn't understand how school works and that you don't blab on really big kids. It's not easy to say that, because I'm basically admitting that I'm a wimp.

I wish, wish, wish I had never raised my hand to be team captain.

"Have these big kids threatened you?"

I shake my head.

"Do you want me to talk to the principal?"

I shake my head again, even harder. That would be the worst thing she could do.

"Then what do you think you need to do?"

"I don't know," I admit.

"If you know someone did something wrong, is it your responsibility to speak up about it?"

I just stare at my feet and think about her question. I don't know what to say.

"And you are the team captain," she continues. "It's up to you to set an example for your classmates."

I continue to stare at the floor, feeling all squirmy inside.

"Just remember," Mom says, "that it's always best to be honest and open."

"I know that, Mom."

"Are you sure?"

I nod. "But it's not that simple."

"Well, I have faith in you. And I have faith that you'll do the right thing." She kisses me on the forehead and then gives me a hug, and I let her hug me because we're not in a school office, so there's no one to see.

I just wish I felt as confident about me as she does about me.

16
LILLY

After dinner, I'm on the phone with Sarah. She's excited, gloating about our plan today and how it is so unfair we weren't declared winners.

I say "Uh-huh" and "Right," but mostly she talks, and I think it's easier to gloat about cheating when you didn't lose your best friend a few hours earlier like I did.

"So what's the plan tomorrow?" she asks me.

"Maybe we just win by winning?" I suggest.

She laughs a short, nasty laugh. "Good one," she says, as if I told a great joke. "Did you see the look on Team Blue's faces when they saw all the balloons were filled with the same pudding? It was the best look ever."

"They looked angry."

"Losers always look angry," she says. "That's because . . ."

"Losing is for losers," I say before she says it, because I know that's exactly what she is going to say.

When I got my sleeping bag from Adventure Scouts, and Francine Pepper discovered I didn't actually own a unicorn, she never spoke to me again. Francine moved away that next year, so I never apologized or thanked her or anything.

I wonder if George will never speak to me again.

Does that make Francine Pepper a loser? Or George? Or maybe me?

Sarah says that she hates talking on the phone because phone talking is stupid, and I need to get a cell phone because everyone texts, and I can't continue to be friends with her and Grace if I can't text. She says that she might have a sleepover and if she does, maybe I'll be invited, but I'll need a phone. Mom and Dad say I can't get one until seventh grade, and that's a long way away, so I guess I'm not invited to her sleepover and maybe I won't have any friends at all after this week.

We end our phone call without any plans to cheat tomorrow, which is a good thing, I guess.

Maybe if we don't cheat, George and I can be friends again. Or maybe we'll be friends again if I give him a ride on a unicorn.

I think about making a clay unicorn, because making things with clay sometimes makes me feel better about things, but instead I lie on my bed and bury my head in my pillow.

17

GEORGE

I pass Abraham Lincoln on the sidewalk near school. He tips his tall black top hat to me. "Four score and seven years ago," he bellows in an odd western voice, but I don't think Abraham Lincoln was from the West. Walking with him is Amelia Earhart, or maybe it's Bessie Coleman. At least I think it's one of them, because Giovanna wears a flight suit and goggles, and I can't think of any other famous women who wore a flight suit and goggles.

Today's Spirit Week contest is Historical Figure Day. We're all dressed as historical figures. I'm Albert Einstein. My costume was easy to put together, because Mom had this old wig that she no longer wears, so I cut the hair shorter and made it all messy and stand up straight. Albert Einstein had goofy hair. I also carry a test tube and wear a lab coat, since Einstein was a scientist, and I drew a fake bushy mustache under my nose. I hope the marker won't be hard to wash off, since I'd hate to walk around with a fake marker mustache for a few days.

I tried washing a little off with my hand sanitizer, and it didn't work at all. I doubt marker chemicals are good for your skin, either.

I spy Cleopatra. She walks on the sidewalk on the other side of the street. It's Lilly. Her outfit impresses me. She obviously spent some effort finding a long white gown and an Egyptian headdress. She even wears a black wig. "Great costume," I shout, but I don't think she heard me. I'm glad she didn't hear me, because I remembered too late that we're not friends anymore, so I shouldn't compliment her.

It feels strange not walking with Lilly when there she is, striding along the opposite side of the street.

I cross the street at the crosswalk. Mr. Whipple, the crossing guard, waves me across. "Hi, Al," he says.

"It's me, George," I say, but then I realize Al is short for Albert, as in Albert Einstein. "I mean, hello," I mumble.

In front of the school, the entire walkway is filled with fifth graders in costumes. Luke waves to me, a saxophone strapped around his shoulders. He puts his lips to his mouthpiece and plays a few notes. He's pretty good.

"I'm Charlie Parker," he explains. "The all-time greatest saxophone player. I've taken sax lessons since I was little." He plays a few more notes.

I had no idea Luke played music. Maybe that's why he's bouncing all the time.

As we walk toward the school entrance, I wave to Eric. He is dressed as George Washington. "Hi, Mr. President," I say.

"Nncllzqk," Eric grunts. I can't understand a word he says through his oversized wooden teeth. He grimaces. The teeth look painful to wear. I wonder if George's Washington's teeth really looked so weird.

Everyone on Team Blue is in costume, at least everyone I see standing in front of the school. That brings a big grin to my face. I'm sure we'll win today's contest, and we need the victory to even things up with Team Red. I called half the team last night and sent a text to the other half, and many kids texted back which costume they planned to wear today. Some sent selfies.

Not every outfit is great, though. Samantha walks by, insisting she is dressed as Annie Oakley, the famous western sharpshooter. But she wears a fancy dress, sparkly shoes, and a matching purse. She says she dressed how Annie Oakley would have dressed for a fancy dinner party. I'm not sure if the judges will agree.

But I still have a smile on my face because I see a whole Team Red group walk past us, and none of them wear costumes. That's probably because Lilly forgot to remind everyone on her team.

"I think we're going to win this," Luke whispers to me, his legs bouncing with excitement. He toots a few notes on his sax.

"We're winning today, that much is plain. Any other idea is simply insane," rhymes Kyle. He's dressed as William Shakespeare with a fake beard and a fancy frock with a big collar. He continues rhyming, "On the stage I'm not going solo. I'll have Soda, dressed as Marco Polo."

"Great!" I say. Soda is Mrs. Rosenbloom's class hamster. Having her in a costume is a terrific idea.

"Kwwllkc quwlzk," says Eric through his wooden teeth. He spits them out and massages his gums. "Sorry. I mean, I cannot tell a lie, since I'm George Washington. We're going to win."

I just need to make sure Lilly doesn't spill her breakfast on me or on my teammates and ruin our costumes. That's just the sort of devious scheme she would pull.

"I hear the winner gets a year's supply of comic books," says Eric.

"I hear we win season tickets to an amusement park," says Luke.

"Which one?" I ask.

"Every one!" exclaims Luke.

Brian approaches us. He walks with big angry strides, but he always walks that way. He wears a mask and an orange shirt and giant red claws on his hands. On his feet are big black boots.

"Uh, we're supposed to be dressed up as historical figures," says Eric.

"I'm Lobster Man," he says. "That's a historical figure."

"You're who?" asks Eric.

"Lobster Man," Brian declares. He holds out his claws and yells, "Lobster Power!"

"Actually, Eric is right about . . . ," I begin.

"Right about what?" Brian demands, curling his lobster claws into fists.

"Nothing, it's a great costume," I quickly say with an awkward smile. Then I add, "I like bikes." I grimace when I say that last part.

As we walk into school, Brian turns to me. "Don't worry, I have a plan. You're with us, right?"

I remember my discussion with Mom last night, and I know I should speak up and say I'm not with him and whatever he's planning. But I look at Brian, who seems even bigger in his lobster costume, and instead I wither like a dead weed. "Of course. One hundred percent with you," I mumble.

"Because we need to teach Team Red a lesson."

"You bet," I say as we walk into the school, hoping his plan is as half-baked as his costume. I think we're going to win, fair and square. We don't need to cheat.

18
LILLY

While I put my stuff into my locker, Finn laughs a single "Ha!" He's not standing next to me, but it's a loud "Ha" that's hard to miss. It's the sort of laugh you have when you're bigger than almost anyone else so you don't care if anyone knows you're laughing. It's not a funny laugh, but a sort of nasty one, and I don't like it very much. He and Grace are huddled next to her locker, so I suspect the laugh is definitely nasty. Grace sees me. "Hey!" She waves me to join them.

Finn is dressed as a pirate, and Grace is dressed like a nun. Finn seems like the pirate type, but Grace does not seem nun-like.

"I'm Mother Teresa," explains Grace, twirling around. "She was famous for doing good deeds. She did lots of them."

No, Grace's costume does not seem right for her at all.

"What's up?" I ask.

"Just talking about what needs to be done to Team Blue," says Grace.

"I heard the winner of Spirit Week gets an entire truck of french fries. And a second truck of ketchup," adds Finn. He sounds excited.

Grace shakes her head. "I don't like ketchup."

Finn frowns and looks down at his toes.

Personally, I would love my own french-fry truck with extra ketchup, and just thinking about it makes my legs want to bounce and jump, but I'm not sure if I believe that will be the prize. I'm also less interested in imaginary french-fry trucks than I am in what the two of them are planning. "What are you guys thinking of doing?"

"We're not sure," admits Grace.

"Maybe I can get them to walk the plank," says Finn the pirate.

"Where would you get a plank?" I ask.

Finn shrugs. "That's part of the problem."

"But Finn's going to help us," adds Grace.

Finn nods. "Grace says I get to ride her horse if I help you guys cheat."

I scrunch my nose and shake my head. I'm positive Grace doesn't own a horse, and memories of my unicorn promise to Francine Pepper flood my brain. I should say something, but Grace winks at me and I keep quiet.

I hate myself for saying nothing, but I still want to win, and Finn could help us win, and at least I'm not the one doing the lying. Also, maybe this means I can still sleep over at Sarah's house even without owning a phone.

I look around the hallway. Every kid on Team Blue wears a costume of some sort. Some outfits I recognize, like pilgrims and American Revolution heroes. But some kids wear dress shirts and ties or fancy dresses, and they could be almost anyone who was rich or famous from whenever or wherever.

Koko sticks her head into our small circle. I didn't see her approach us. She's dressed in old-timey clothes with an old-timey camera hanging around her neck. I must look confused, because she says, "I'm Dorothea Lange, the photographer. But why doesn't Lilly just spill milk and oatmeal on everyone? That worked last time."

"It was an accident," I insist.

Mother Teresa, or rather Grace, pats me on the back. "Sure it was." She winks.

Aisha pops her head into our growing circle. She wears a track outfit. She called me last night and told me she was dressing as Jackie Joyner-Kersee, a famous Olympic athlete. "What are you guys doing?"

"Plotting," says Grace.

Aisha frowns, shakes her head, and walks away.

"I can make them all disappear," says Pete, who is dressed in a top hat and a cape. "I'm Harry Houdini, a famous magician."

"I can make them all sick," says Amelia. She's dressed in rags. "I'm Typhoid Mary. She was sort of famous for making people sick."

"Um, great costume," I say but thinking the opposite and suddenly wishing George was next to me so I could borrow his hand sanitizer.

Thinking of George makes my stomach sink, and I push his face out of my brain. "Good ideas, guys. But I'm not sure any of those things will work."

Our circle of plotters is now four people deep.

"Let's hypnotize the judges into voting for us," says Pete. "I've been reading about hypnosis. I hypnotized my dog once."

"How could you tell?" I ask.

Pete shrugs. "Well, I think I hypnotized my dog once."

"Let's build a time machine and go back into history and change stuff so there aren't any more historical figures and Team Blue won't be dressed as anyone," says Zachary. I can't tell if he's joking or serious. He seems serious. He's dressed as a mobster from the 1920s with a fake scar down his cheek.

"What if we tell Team Blue the judging has moved to a different building?" says Noah. He's holding a dictionary, and

I heard he's dressed as Noah Webster, who I think wrote the very first dictionary in America. "Or two buildings. Or just tell them the event is canceled. Or change the clocks so they are late, or something different than those ideas."

"Let's steal their shoes," suggests Grace. "And their socks! And put thumbtacks on the ground so they can't walk on the stage."

"Or we can steal the stage!" Koko says excitedly.

Our circle is still growing and people are shouting out ideas that make no sense at all. It's like everyone wants to cheat, but is not sure how. I wonder if, maybe, we should try to win without cheating.

Ugh, I sound like George. I really need to get his head out of my head.

I remove my black Cleopatra wig. It's itchy, and I hope that's how my George thoughts keep popping in, through the itchiness.

As I take off my wig, I look down at my wrist. I only wore the friendship bracelet for a few days, but my wrist looks weird without it. I had been so excited when I made them. I know George and I ended our friendship just yesterday, but I miss having a best friend, and it already seems like forever since we talked. I remember what our parents said right before this whole week started. They said that no contest is more important than friendship.

I will find George and tell him I'm sorry for everything. I'll tell him I knew about the pudding plot, and I'm sorry and I miss him and ask him to forgive me. We'll walk home together today, and everything will be just like it used to be.

I'll tell him that I'm sorry right after we win the costume contest, though. Sure, we don't have a scheme to guarantee victory, but I still want to win that free french-fry truck, or whatever prize will be handed out, and it's easier to apologize when you're a winner.

19
GEORGE

As I push through the doors of the fifth-grade hallway, I don't spot Lilly. Her locker is near the front of the hall, so I usually see her right away. I'm feeling guilty for the way I've been acting and the things that I've been thinking. Sure, she started this whole mess by ruining my Twin Day outfit. Still, just because someone does something mean to you, that doesn't mean you need to do something mean back. How you act is up to you. I can choose to act nicer.

I do choose to act nicer.

But then I notice Lilly. A giant circle of Team Red kids huddle together, and Lilly is right in the middle of them. I can see the top of her bright red head peeking out. She must have taken off her wig.

Lilly and I will talk later, when less people are around. I'll ask her to look me in the eye and be honest with me. Is she behind any of this?

And if she says no, I'll believe her.

And if she says yes, maybe I'll forgive her anyway.

From the corner of my eye, I see someone waving to me from the hallway behind me. I need to get to my locker because class starts soon. But it's hard to ignore a waving hand. So I walk out the doors of the fifth-grade hall.

But I'm anxious to turn around and get to class.

Brian still wears his Lobster Man outfit. "Come here! Quick! Quietly!" he shouts, which sort of ruins the whole idea of being quiet. But no one else is near to hear. Everyone is already filing into his or her room.

"Follow me," orders Brian. He walks briskly ahead, down the hall that leads to the cafeteria. There are no classrooms in this corridor, just closets and maintenance rooms. It's empty except for us.

"We need to get back," I say. "Or we'll be late."

"No time," he says, and I have to jog to keep up with him. We approach the cafeteria door. Brian looks both ways to make sure we're alone.

The hairs on the back of my neck stand up.

"I don't think we're allowed in here," I warn, but Brian has already removed a key from his pocket and inserted it into the lock on the door. He twists the key and pushes the door open.

"My older brother Simon works in the cafeteria," says Brian.

"Does he know you have his key?"

Brian smiles. "He's on our side, don't worry."

The cafeteria is empty. It's already been cleaned from breakfast, but I guess it is too early to serve lunch. It smells like eggs.

Brian walks past the lunch tables. I hurry to keep up. "Where are we going?"

Brian doesn't answer. He marches across the lunchroom and through the swinging door that leads to the kitchen.

I have never been inside the kitchen. I don't think kids are allowed here, and I expect to see the angry face of Principal Klein hiding behind a counter, ready to drag me to his office.

I don't want to go back to his office. I don't want to be team captain. I don't want to be here. I want to go to class.

The kitchen looks clean, crammed with stainless-steel counters and shiny white floors that look recently mopped. But the smell of eggs hits my nose like a soccer ball. I scrunch up my nostrils to keep as much stink out as I can. I want to wipe my nose with hand sanitizer.

"Howdy," Seth says in a southern drawl. He sits on the kitchen floor wearing a cowboy hat and vest. "James is the name. Jesse James. Most ruthless gunslinger in the West."

Next to Seth is an older kid that I can only assume is Brian's brother. He looks like Brian, but with a goatee.

"This is your captain?" Brian's brother asks, looking at me with a sneer. "Doesn't look like much."

Brian nods. "He's okay, and he's no snitch." He points to his brother. "Simon was on Team Blue back when he was in fifth grade."

"We lost," says Simon. His voice has the same tinge of anger that I often hear in Brian's voice. "But we're not losing this year. No way I'm letting my little bro lose to Team Red."

Large woolen blankets lie in heaps around them, and next to those is a giant drum of what looks to be yellowish slime. I peer closer into the drum and the strong egg odor makes my eyes water.

"Egg salad," says Brian with glee. I have no idea why egg salad would make anyone so happy. "Isn't this stuff awful?"

I nod my head.

"We have forty pounds of it," says Simon. "There are three more containers in back. But don't worry, no one will notice anything is missing." He points to himself and says proudly, "I keep track of the inventory and everything. It's an important job."

Brian peers into the egg-salad bucket with a grin.

I'm struggling to breathe, and I wonder how Brian can stand the odor, but it doesn't seem to bother him. "So, um, what are you guys doing with forty pounds of egg salad? Making lunch? Planning a picnic?"

Simon laughs as if I've made a joke. "We're doing what needs to be done." To Seth, he barks, "Stir it so it's nice and goopy, Jesse James."

Seth stirs the drum with a long spatula. "I hear the winner of Spirit Week gets a year without homework." Seth takes a big whiff of the barrel. I think he actually enjoys the stink.

"I heard it's two years without homework," says Brian, who also inhales the egg smell with a happy smile. Meanwhile, I have to hide my nose in my arm to keep the odor away.

"All I know is that Team Red is about to get what's coming to them," says Simon.

"They have egg salad coming to them?" I ask, holding my breath.

Simon laughs again and puts out his palm. "Hit me, little bro." Brian meets it with a loud hand slap. "There's no way you guys lose today."

"What are you guys up to?" I ask, my voice rising along with my worry. "You're not going to pour this inside lockers, are you? Principal Klein said . . ."

"We've been there, done that," says Brian. "This plan is way better."

"Do we have enough blankets?" Simon asks. Seth unfolds two of the blankets. They are large and unfold and unfold. They must fit on some giant bed.

Maybe they plan on making a bed filled with egg salad.

No, that makes no sense.

"I think we have more than enough blankets," says Seth.

Then the school bell rings.

"I should get to class," I say. I take a few steps toward the door, eager to get away from the smell and the stink of whatever rotten thing they are planning. But then I stop.

I'm the team captain. I think of my conversation with Mom. I think of how I promised everyone I would play fair. I don't know what's going on here, but whatever it is, it is not good.

Keeping silent is just as bad as doing bad things.

I turn around. I take a deep breath, which is not easy with the horrible smell of egg salad. I face Seth, Brian, and Simon. "Guys?"

"What?" asks Simon, glaring at me.

They are so much bigger than me that I gulp twice before I continue. "Well, you know, Principal Klein says we're supposed to display good sports . . ." My voice catches in my throat. Speaking out is not easy.

"Good sports?" asks Brian, confused.

I cough. ". . . manship. Principal Klein says we're supposed to, you know, display good sportsmanship. That's what I meant."

They all frown, Simon deepest of all. "I thought you said he was okay," he says to Brian, eyeing me warily.

"I thought he was," growls Brian.

Neither of them looks happy with me, but this is where I put my foot down. This is where I earn my I LOVE GOLDFISH! badge. "Right, good sportsmanship. So, you know, whatever you're going to do with that egg salad, maybe you shouldn't?" I gulp and cough and smile. If I smile really, really wide, maybe they won't do anything terrible to me.

They are all so very, very big.

Why did I volunteer for team captain?

"He's going to ruin everything," says Simon, with a scowl.

"I just wanted to remind you guys of the sportsmanship thing," I say. "And you know I like bikes." I hate myself for saying that last part, since it makes no sense. I smile again.

"If he tells anyone, I could get sacked," says Simon, who is not returning my smile. "And I have an important job."

"He won't tell anyone," says Brian. He stares at me. "Right? You said you were with us."

"Right. Of course. One hundred percent," I say. "But I'm the team captain, and I don't know if—"

Simon interrupts me. "We shouldn't talk about it here." I look around the room. There is no one here but the four of us. "Over there," says Simon, waving me across the room.

I shrug and follow him across the kitchen.

We walk past sinks and a large cooler to what I think might be a closet. Simon puts his hand on the doorknob. "In here."

I guess Simon wants our conversation to be extra private. Maybe he wants to admit he's wrong but is embarrassed to say it in front of Brian and Seth. He opens the door.

"I'm glad you agree that . . . ," I begin, as I take a step forward.

I don't even finish the words. Simon pushes me forward. I stumble, and Simon slams the door shut.

I hear him yell, "He can stay there until we're done!"

I race forward and reach for the knob. The door is locked. "Hey! Let me out!"

No one answers.

I bang on the door.

Nothing.

Thankfully, there is an overhead fluorescent light so I can see where I am. If it was completely dark, I think I would start screaming. The closet is filled with tall shelves that house boxes of ketchup and mustard, and plastic bags filled with sandwich breads, and jars of sauces. At least I won't starve. But I'm helpless to stop whatever those guys have planned.

I so hate being team captain.

20
LILLY

The entire grade files into the school auditorium at lunchtime. Food isn't usually allowed in here, but it's a special week and they ordered pizza, although we're supposed to be extra careful. The usual cafeteria pizza tastes like cardboard with fake cheese, but the school brought in Rosa's Pizza for us. Rosa's is the pizza we order at home, so this is the best school lunch ever.

I sit near the middle of the auditorium, one hand holding my paper plate filled with pizza goodness, and my other hand holding a cup of apple juice. Everything tastes so good I can't help but bounce on my seat, although I splash a little apple juice on my pants, so I try to keep my legs from moving so much.

I sit between Aisha and Sarah. Grace sits next to Sarah.

Sarah has three pieces of pizza on her plate. We were only supposed to grab two pieces each. "I'm a queen, so I can eat whatever I want," she says. Sarah wears a plain blue dress with glitter glued on it, and a cheap tinfoil tiara.

"Whatever you say, Queen," I reply.

"Please address me as 'Your Royal Highness,'" Sarah says with a snooty and dirty look, as if she's royalty and I'm most definitely not. She fluffs her hair. "I'm Queen Mary." Sarah throws a mischievous glance. "As Queen of England, she's considered one of the most ruthless queens in history. She did all sorts of horrible things. Just like we're going to do horrible things to Team Blue."

"Well, maybe not so horrible, right?" I say with a small laugh, but my small laugh is met with stone-cold silence.

I feel something wet and slimy smack against the back of my neck. I quickly reach around and remove a piece of pepperoni that has stuck to my skin like tape.

I turn to see Brian and Seth, five rows in back of me, chucking pepperoni slices at our team while laughing. We were supposed to be careful when eating here, but they don't seem to care. One slice hits Pete in the head. Pete turns around and glares. He is in his Harry Houdini outfit, and I bet he wishes he could perform some sort of disappearing magic on them right now. Seth and Brian both hold a stack of pepperonis that they probably swiped from half the kids on their team.

But before they can launch another volley of meat at us, Principal Klein's bellowing voice reverberates through the room. "Seth and Brian, put down the pepperoni and step into the hallway. Now."

The bullies' smiles vanish as Principal Klein marches down the aisle. They scoot out from their seats to follow, and I want to shout out, "It serves you right!" but I just think it really loudly instead.

Seth wears a cowboy outfit, but Brian is dressed as a weird lobster superhero.

"We should win this contest because we didn't throw pepperoni," says Sarah.

"They're just a couple of idiots," I say.

Sarah shakes her head. "It's a whole team of idiots and cheaters. Brian and Seth just do most of the dirty work."

On the stage in front of us, three judges sit behind a long table waiting for our principal to return. One of the judges is my teacher, Mrs. Crawford, and I hope that she'll want us to win and give us extra judging points. She is dressed as a pilgrim.

Next to her is Mr. Foley, who is George's teacher, and I worry that he might give Team Blue extra points. I guess he and Mrs. Crawford sort of even themselves out. Mr. Foley is dressed in a business suit and has large white sideburns curled almost to his mouth. Someone told me he is supposed to be John Quincy Adams, who was our sixth president, but I don't know why someone would dress as John Quincy Adams when there are so many more famous presidents to choose. The only thing I know about John Quincy Adams is that he was related to John Adams, who was a more famous president, and that he's in our school history book with three names, while most of our other presidents only have two names.

The last judge on stage is older and wears a three-piece suit and a long fake nose. I'm not sure who he is, although he looks sort of familiar, and he talks with the other teachers with big arm flourishes. The other teachers seem sort of annoyed that he talks so much. They nod and smile, but the smiles are obviously pretend.

Aisha takes a big sniff and scrunches her nose. "Do you smell eggs?"

I take a big whiff, too. "Maybe. Gross."

"It seems strange to be smelling eggs, doesn't it?"

Principal Klein returns through the auditorium doors. They slam shut behind him, and he briskly stomps down the aisle. He walks alone, with purpose, his hands swinging. Seth and Brian must be in big trouble, ordered to wait in the principal's office or in prison or somewhere. They are not with him.

As I look around the room, I notice an entire row of Team Red kids who forgot to dress up. They wear what they always wear to school. I suddenly worry that we might not win this contest. Sarah follows my eyes and frowns at me. "Nice planning," she says, dripping with sarcasm. "Maybe you should have texted someone. Oh, right. You don't have a phone."

I know I didn't tell anyone to wear costumes today, but kids should have been able to remember that today is Historical Figure Day without my reminding them. The schedule is posted in every classroom.

"If we lose, do I still get to ride your horse?" Finn asks Grace. He sits behind us.

"Never," says Grace, coldly.

Finn pouts.

Principal Klein walks up the stage steps and to the microphone. "Sorry for the delay, but we are ready to begin." He takes a deep breath, as if trying to exhale any anger that lingers from the pepperoni throwing. "I'm thrilled to announce a special guest to help judge our costumes. Some of you might already know Mr. Wolcott. He was just named the new head of drama at Liberty Falls Community College."

The old guy with the fake nose waves, and a large cheer goes up from the kids in Mrs. Rosenbloom's class. They must know him. He says, "Remember, as the bard himself says, 'All the world's a stage, and all the men and women merely players.'"

I have no idea what he's talking about. The other judges clap politely, although I don't think they know what he's talking about, either.

"Team Blue, please approach the stage," orders Principal Klein.

Half the kids—all of Team Blue—stand up and make their way to the aisle. They march up the stage steps, where they will walk past the judges for scoring. Each judge has a pad of paper to make notes.

I look for George. I still can't get his face out of my brain, but I don't see him.

Where is he?

Up on stage, kids file past the judges in a wide variety of costumes. Some of the getups were obviously put on at the last minute, like a few kids in baseball caps and team jerseys, a couple of which have names taped to the back for famous ball players. But other costumes are pretty great, and either took a lot of time to create or to find in a costume store. Gavin's Abraham Lincoln is almost perfect, from the fake beard to the black suit and hat. Jamaal wears a long black judge's robe. I hear he's dressed as Thurgood Marshall, who was the first African American Supreme Court justice.

Kyle, dressed in some silly outfit with a big white collar, walks past the judges. He holds Soda, their class hamster, who he's dressed in a fake beard, a small furry hat, and a red robe.

It's a nice touch. I wish I had thought of dressing up our class turtle, Elvis, as someone historic.

When the last member of Team Blue leaves the stage, Principal Klein announces, "Wonderful costumes. All the judges are quite impressed. Team Red, please come up."

I leap out of my seat, my fingers crossed, but still wondering: Where is George?

21

GEORGE

I'm not sure how long I've been in this closet. It feels like hours. I almost opened a jar of pickles to eat, but that would be like stealing, so I didn't.

I spent some time reorganizing the shelves. There were some garbanzo beans mixed in with jars of roasted red peppers by accident, and I really thought the condiments should be in alphabetical order.

I put ketchup under *K* even though the jars say *catsup*. The inconsistency bothers me, but I think my filing system makes the most sense.

The doorknob turns. I crouch, expecting to see Simon and Brian, and who knows what they have planned. I'm not a fighter, and I'm not fast, so my best chance of escape is to throw a handful of flour at them. Then, while the white cloud blinds them, I can make a break for it.

I hold a sack of flour, top open, ready.

The door opens.

"Oh!" exclaims one of the lunch ladies, standing in the doorway. But I have already thrown a fistful of flour at her before I realize she's not Simon or Brian.

As she coughs and swipes the air and rubs her eyes, I make my move, dashing past her and through the flour cloud. "Sorry, sorry, sorry," I call out as I run. "And I filed catsup under *K*!"

Then I'm off, racing across the room and banging the kitchen door open.

As I dash across the cafeteria, I look up at the clock. It's lunchtime. The costume judging has already begun and is probably going on right now. Whatever Brian and Seth and Simon have planned may have already happened.

But maybe not; maybe I can still stop it if I hurry.

I sprint down the hall. My sneakers squeak. The auditorium is just two hallways away. Still, when I arrive and push open the auditorium doors, I'm breathing heavily from running.

I am not too late. Team Red is on stage, walking in front of the judges. Lilly leads her group, and nothing terrible seems to have happened. It is calm in here. Too calm. I scan the room, but I'm not sure what I'm looking to find.

Then I see them. Blankets. Big woolen blankets hang from the rafters, stretched wide above the stage, tied in place with ropes. The middles of the blankets sag, as if weighted with something heavy.

A foot peeks out from behind a curtain, way in the back of the stage where no one should be standing. It's a black boot, like something a lobster superhero might wear.

Then, like a lightbulb brightening over my head, suddenly I know exactly what's going to happen.

I yell as loudly as I can, "Run! Egg salad!"

But it's too late, because the moment I scream it, and just as everyone in the entire room turns to me and wonders what I'm talking about and why I'm standing near the front doors and where I've been this whole time, the overhead ropes are loosened and the blankets fall from above. With them, forty pounds of egg salad drench the stage and nearly every member of Team Red.

22
LILLY

I am soaked in eggs.

No. I am soaked in egg salad. This is most definitely egg salad.

To make things even worse, not that anything could be much worse, I hate egg salad.

My hair stinks with eggs and mayo. My arms stink with eggs and mayo. My everything and everywhere stinks with eggs and mayo.

Tara stands next to me, shivering. She wore a toga, dressed as a famous Greek philosopher, which means she's basically just wearing a fancy bedsheet and a leotard under it, so she was probably cold anyway, but now huge clumps of cold egg salad cling to her hair and shoulders. I think she got the worst of it.

Or maybe Sarah got the worst of it. Or maybe Alex got it worse. Or Noah. Or me.

Wet egg-puddle muck surrounds our feet. I step forward,

and my shoes plop in the goop. But the smell is the worst part of it.

The egg salad avoided the judges, though. They are clean. Whoever planned this mess, planned it well. But there is no questioning who planned it.

"Someone is going to pay for this!" yells Finn. For a moment, I'm scared because he looks crazy, like a wild beast. His pirate outfit, covered in egg salad as if he lost some sort of egg-salad pirate battle, just adds to his scariness.

"Oh yeah, they'll pay," echoes Zane. He tries to look fierce, but he can't because his eyes are too kind to ever look fierce, and because he's dressed as Bozo the Clown. (Some clowns are scary, but Zane's Bozo outfit is not.) I'm not even sure if Bozo the Clown really counts as a historical figure, not that it matters anymore.

Jessie, who is dressed as Marie Antoinette, sobs and asks, "Do they hate cats?" She told me earlier that Marie Antoinette loved cats.

"If Team Blue wants war, we'll give them war," growls Mother Teresa, I mean Grace, wiping egg slop from her nun habit. She hisses, but I don't think the real Mother Teresa would have ever hissed.

I heard something right before we were drenched with egg mess. Someone yelled something from the audience, and I think it was George.

Yes, it was George. He yelled, "Egg salad!" He knew this was going to happen. He was in on the plan. Maybe it was even his idea.

I'm so mad at him. I can't believe he'd do something so terrible. Especially when he knows how much I hate egg salad.

And to think I wanted to be friends with him again! I can't believe I've been feeling guilty about cheating and fighting with him, and even thought about apologizing to him.

Pete grunts. Grace snarls. Jessie roars like a big cat.

"Who did this?" Principal Klein cries. He stands near me. His suit pants have a clop of egg salad on the bottom. He bends down and brushes it off with a flick of his finger, the chunk of salad flying a few feet and landing next to me. "I said, who did this?" He stares at me, and then across our entire team. But he can't think one of us did this to ourselves.

"As the great bard William Shakespeare himself once wrote, 'That one may smile, and smile, and be a villain,'" says Mr. Wolcott from the judges' table. The other judges ignore him.

Principal Klein's face is red and his large hands shake as he scans the audience. Team Blue watches us, their jaws hanging open. I think they are too stunned to speak.

But one kid stands out. One kid, standing in the way back of the auditorium, has *guilty* plastered on his face.

"This can't continue and it won't!" yells Principal Klein, his voice exploding in anger. "Shame on you all!"

Someone starts sobbing, the crying spreading through the now otherwise silent auditorium. The only other sound in the room is a plop, plop, plop of egg salad from a clump high up on the rafters continuing to drop on the floor.

"Someone will answer for this," says Principal Klein, now in an eerie and calm voice that's even scarier than when he yelled. His hands are clenched into claws as if he wants to strangle something. Then his arm shoots out and points to the only kid standing in the room. "George Martinez. You!"

George, who stood straight a moment ago, appears to be suddenly made of gelatin. His legs quake and he leans against the auditorium door as if he can't stand on his own.

"Come to my office right now, George Martinez," says Principal Klein, the veins in his neck nearly popping out. He stomps across the stage and down the stairs.

George peels himself off the door when Principal Klein approaches him and stands at attention, ready to follow him out of the room.

I snort, and that's not something I meant to do or do very often, but it is a snort of satisfaction. George deserves whatever punishment he gets, the bigger the better.

Before they walk out the door our principal wheels around, as if suddenly yanked by a string. He looks up to the stage and his eyes rest on me, Cleopatra, Queen of the Nile, Queen of Egg Salad. His eyes are large and wide. His expression is menacing.

"And Lilly Bloch. You come with us, too."

"But . . . ," I say.

"Now!" our principal bellows.

I trudge across the stage, down the steps, and march down the aisle. All eyes watch me.

"Please get these kids cleaned up," Principal Klein calls back to the judges. "Hopefully most kids brought a change of clothes." Then I hear a big clop of egg salad fall from high above the stage and land on the floor. It's the last sound I hear before the auditorium doors swing shut behind us.

23
GEORGE

So here I am, again, in Principal Klein's tiny office. This time, Lilly sits next to me. Mrs. Frank brought in a folding chair for Lilly to sit on, and there is barely room for us across from our principal's desk. Our knees bump each other. Principal Klein's face is as red as a fire engine, and I wouldn't be all that surprised to hear a fire alarm ring out from his nose. He does not sit, but paces in the small space behind his deck, two steps one way and then two steps back, back and forth, back and forth. As he talks, his hands, his incredibly large hands, ball into fists and continually punch the air.

"I have never, in all my years as principal, seen such horrible, terrible, and irresponsible behavior!" he rants. "Poor sportsmanship! A total disregard for decency and rules! I am ashamed, yes, ashamed to be your principal."

"My team had nothing to do with this," says Lilly. "It was all George . . ."

"Quiet!" bellows Principal Klein. "Not a word from either one of you."

"Yes, sir," I say, and I guess that counts as a word from one of us because Principal Klein glares at me and holds his finger up, as if warning me that *one more time* and I will be in even more boatloads of trouble than I am already. I keep quiet.

Our principal continues his small-step pacing. "Spirit Week is about teamwork and caring and doing our best." Fist punch. "This is an embarrassment to me, to the fifth grade, and to the entire school." Two more fist punches. "You've left me no choice. None. Spirit Week is over." Three more fist punches, followed by a sort of karate chop. "No more contests. No more events. No more fun. Instead, the entire fifth grade will serve detention after school today. Mrs. Frank will be calling all of your parents." He juts his fist straight up in the air and then points directly at me. "And, George, I am especially disappointed in you."

I open my mouth to proclaim my innocence, but I've already been warned to keep quiet, so I close my mouth and say nothing as our principal continues.

"George, I warned you there would be consequences. It seems obvious that Team Blue committed this horrendous act. I am suspending you from school, effective immediately."

My jaw drops open. Even though we are forbidden from speaking, my voice flows out of my throat before I can stop it.

"But, sir, I had nothing to do with it. Honestly, sir. Please. You can't suspend me."

Principal Klein—who looks even angrier than Lilly did when I beat her at tic-tac-toe the other week, ruining her streak of 228 wins in a row (although I lost a lot of them on purpose to keep her streak going)—stops pacing and stares at me, and stares and stares, and after about twenty seconds of staring, the veins in his neck ebb just ever so slightly. His face turns a less vibrant shade of red.

"I swear I didn't know," I gulp.

"I hear you were missing from class this morning. And you weren't on stage during Team Blue's costume presentation. And then you appeared and yelled something right before it happened, didn't you?" he asks, his voice still tinged with anger. "It sounded like *egg salad*. It seems strange, in fact it seems impossible, that you would just yell out the words *egg salad* for no reason."

He has a point, but I have a witness. Except I can't tell him that because then Principal Klein will want to know how I got trapped in the closet. I gulp and instead say, "Well, uh, I left part of my costume at home. So then I had to run home, and then run back, and then I went the wrong way, so I was late." I feel my face turn red, but I keep talking. "When I got to the auditorium, I saw blankets with egg salad up on the rafters. I noticed they were about to fall. I wanted to warn everyone."

"You could see blankets from all the way in the back of the auditorium?"

I nod.

He leans over his desk and stares at me, as if willing my thoughts to jump out of my head and land on his table, which is cluttered with pens.

I really, really want to put the pens in his pen jar.

"And you could see these blankets were filled with egg salad?" he asks. "How is that possible?"

I take a deep breath. If I tell him the truth, then I'm a snitch, and I'll have to hide in the halls every time I see Brian or Seth. But if I don't say anything, then I might be expelled. I bite my lip. I fidget.

I told my mom I could handle this. No one is going to help me.

I should just tattle.

I hate being team captain.

But it's not all Brian and Seth's fault. Not entirely. I told Brian I was with him, 100 percent. What did I think he was planning to do? Did I think he was going to bake smiley face cookies for everyone to eat? Of course he wasn't. He was going to do something terrible, and I told him to go ahead and do it.

Even if I spoke up in the end, I didn't speak up soon enough. That makes me sort of guilty, but not really guilty, and not guilty enough to be suspended, I think.

I should get extra bonus points for organizing their food storage closet, at the very least.

I look down at my goldfish pin. I didn't want to be our team captain, but I volunteered, and here I am, and I have to handle this. I take a deep breath. I wonder if I should ask for a lawyer. I put my knees together to stop them from knocking.

"I had nothing to do with it, sir," I mumble. It's all I can think of saying.

"Then who did?" asks Principal Klein.

I bow my head in shame and worry. I keep quiet.

Principal Klein turns to Lilly. I'm sure she's been enjoying every moment watching me squirm. "What do you think, Lilly? Did George have anything to do with the incident?"

Lilly opens her mouth to speak, and I can tell from the slight curl in her mouth that she's going to tell our principal that I'm the sort of person who enjoys hiding egg salad in blankets. But then she looks at me, and her small mouth curl uncurls. Her eyes dash back and forth, so I can tell she's thinking. Her expression turns serious and she shakes her head. "No, sir. I can't imagine George would do that sort of thing. Ever."

My heart, which had been pounding in my chest, quiets a little. I flash her a grateful smile. Of course I would never hatch such a scheme, and of course Lilly would know that.

"So you see, sir, you can't cancel Spirit Week," she continues. "I know a few bad eggs have been ruining things." At the mention of *eggs* our principal's face drops. "Sorry," she mumbles. "But you can't cancel Spirit Week. We've all been trying so hard, and most of us have played by the rules. I mean, you can't punish everyone just because of a few bad eggs, um, I mean apples. Some bad apples." Principal Klein frowns, but he doesn't interrupt her. "And what about the free trip to Disney World we're all going to win? You probably can't get the money back."

Principal Klein looks confused. "Disney World?"

"The prize. The special prize," says Lilly. "I heard it might be Disney World?"

Principal Klein shakes his head. "No, it's not that."

"Please, sir," I add. "Lilly is right. You can't cancel the entire week because of a troublemaker here or there. And I swear I didn't know a thing. I smelled eggs, sir. And I saw the blankets and well, I just figured it out."

"I smelled eggs, too, sir," says Lilly. "And so did Aisha. You can ask her."

"We'll be good," I promise. "I'll make sure of it. And so will Lilly. Both of our teams will play fair, with no more trouble. We swear it."

Lilly nods her head. "We'll all be on our best behavior, sir."

Principal Klein, who had resumed his pacing and is now panting a little from walking back and forth so much, stops and sits down on his leather seat. He spreads his messy pens across his desk so they are even messier.

I grit my teeth and refuse to let myself put the pens back in their jar, even though I really want to.

"I will lift George's suspension," he says, and I breathe a deep sigh of relief. "I can't prove he was responsible, but I suspect he's not being totally honest." He glares at me, but it feels like a giant weight has been lifted from my shoulders. "But I will find out who is responsible for the mess in the auditorium. And that person or persons will be punished." I gulp, and Principal Klein continues. "However, I'm not reversing the rest of it. Spirit Week is canceled and the entire fifth grade will serve detention after school today."

"But . . . ," I begin, and am interrupted by Lilly.

"What about the prize?" she asks.

Our principal responds with a deep frown. "I think there are more important things you should be thinking about right now, like sportsmanship. And responsibility."

We are dismissed from the office and walk past Mrs. Frank's desk. The school secretary frowns at us. Her eyes linger on me. The entire school probably thinks I'm responsible for today's egg-salad incident. I'm relieved that I'm not suspended, but I know I needed to stand up to Brian and Seth. I still need to do something.

I just wish they weren't so much bigger than me.

As we walk out of the office, I hear our principal say to Mrs. Frank behind us: "All this trouble reminds me, did you get me that egg salad recipe? Egg salad is one of my favorite foods, you know."

Lilly shivers. I know how much she dislikes egg salad.

After we open the office door and step into the hallway, I turn to Lilly. "Thanks for sticking up for me." For a moment I think we might be friends again.

But Lilly's face is not friendly. When she speaks, she spits slightly, so I have to step back to avoid spittle. "The only reason I spoke up was to keep him from canceling Spirit Week. I want that prize. But you ruined it. You and your stupid team." She stomps her foot. Egg salad splatters across the floor. "This is not over. Not in the slightest. Spirit Week is continuing as planned. Do you hear me?"

"But Principal Klein said . . ."

"I don't care what he said." She jabs her finger into my chest. "Spirit Week is still on. After what happened today, you owe me. I'm wearing egg salad, George. Egg salad!"

Before I can say anything, she adds, "And we will destroy your team, do you hear me?"

Her eyes lack even a hint of warmth or forgiveness or understanding. I see only dislike and distrust.

But if that's how she wants to be, then I can be that way, too. I meet her glare with one of my own, but it's hard. I don't like glaring. "Beat us? In your dreams."

She jabs me once more in my chest with her finger. "Tomorrow is Pajamas Day. I'll get my team ready, and you get yours. But Team Blue doesn't have a chance."

"But there isn't a Pajamas Day anymore."

"If I say there is Pajamas Day, there's a Pajamas Day." Then, Lilly marches away from me, stomping down the hall. As I stand alone, watching her leave, I wonder why we were best friends in the first place.

But I do know one thing: Team Blue will win Pajamas Day.

24
LILLY

From the cafeteria window, I watch kids leaving school for the day, and I wish I was with them. I stare at a group of second graders racing one another, another group of first graders skipping and holding hands, and a large bunch of fourth graders laughing together as they cross the street to go home.

None of those kids are fifth graders. Our entire grade is stuck serving detention, quietly, which is so unfair because all Team Red did was get doused by egg salad. We should get free laundry, not detention. It's not like we put slime into our lockers and dropped egg salad on ourselves.

At least we get to serve our detention in the cafeteria while Team Blue is stuck in the hot, sock-stinking gym, but they deserve extra heat and extra smelliness.

Fortunately, I wore regular clothes under my costume—a lot of us did, or brought clothes to change into later. Other kids had their parents drop off clean clothes, but a few kids, those who weren't directly under the blankets when they fell, sit on their chairs with a little egg yolk still smeared across their costumes.

While most of us have changed our clothes, our anger hasn't changed at all.

"They got egg in my hair," says Sarah. "My hair!" She fluffs her curly hair, but it doesn't fluff like it usually does. Grace joins her frown, part of her hair as matted down as Sarah's.

"Everyone on Team Blue owes me a horseback ride," says Finn, pouting. He sits across from me at the lunch table, looking at Grace. I shake my head because I still can't believe that he thinks Grace owns a horse. "We need to do something."

"Yes, we do," says Sarah.

I try to think of something terrible, such as sticking lizards inside everyone's pants. I don't know how I will get lizards, or how I can stuff them inside pants, and I don't even like touching lizards since they are wiggly, but I guess that's why pant-stuffing lizards seems so especially mean.

My plan makes no sense.

We could kidnap the entire grade. Or throw paint on them. Or force them to eat the egg salad they poured on us.

All my plans make no sense.

"I think we should . . . ," begins Grace.

"Hush," says Mrs. Greeley. She stands in the middle of the room with her arms folded, looking cross. "Detention means no talking. You are here to learn a lesson, and you will learn that lesson quietly. You will each write a one-page report on the meaning of good sportsmanship. After you are done, you can study or read. But no talking."

I take out a piece of paper and I write, *Good sportsmanship means you'll probably have egg salad dropped on you.*

I push my paper aside. I'm done.

But sitting in the cafeteria for fifty-nine more minutes, without talking, will be almost impossible. I sit still for maybe a minute more, and I'm already fidgeting and bouncing and bored out of my jeans. All I do is think evil thoughts about Team Blue, some involving giant apes and others involving dropping watermelons on them. I wanted to win. I wanted that prize. Team Blue ruined all of it.

I heard Ruby say that the special prize was a guest role on a TV show, which means I could have been discovered, and that would be totally awesomesauce. But now all I get is detention, and detention has no stars.

I think about Pajamas Day and how I told George we would all dress up anyway. That sounded good when I was yelling it in the hallway, but I wasn't really thinking straight. I haven't told any of my teammates what I said to George, but I hope they agree with my plan since it's too late to back out now, not after gloating we would win.

And I won't let George win, prize or no prize.

Mrs. Greeley sits at a table and opens a magazine. I look down at my notebook and draw a flower. I should make a clay flower for my shelf at home. I don't have one of those yet, and a flower seems pretty easy to make, and Mom just bought a whole bunch of clay for me so I could make more frogs, but I have no team to make frogs for anymore. The clock ticks. I draw dogs and cats. I could make some dog and cat figurines, too. With all the clay at home I could make one hundred dogs and cats.

The clock ticks a few million more times.

Mrs. Greeley leans back on her chair. I draw more dogs and more flowers. I don't draw dogs or flowers very well, though. It is easier to make things out of clay.

The clock ticks and tocks. Mrs. Greeley's mouth falls open.

I elbow Sarah and point to Mrs. Greeley. Her eyes are closed and she might even be snoring, just a little. Sarah and I exchange smiles, and so does Grace when she sees what we see.

We whisper, since we don't want to wake up the teacher. "We need to do something to Team Blue," says Sarah.

Grace nods. "They made egg salad. Why don't we just make something more disgusting?"

"I can have my mom make tuna casserole," says Finn, a bit too loudly. "Nothing is worse than my mom's tuna casserole."

"Ssshhh." I point my thumb at Mrs. Greeley.

Our teacher moves her head and I stiffen, but then she's motionless once again.

"They'll be expecting food," I say. "And I doubt your mom would make enough tuna casserole for us to dump on half our grade."

Finn shrugs. "Maybe not. But my mom loves making tuna casserole."

"I can train my cats to bite everyone on Team Blue. Cats are very smart, you know." Jessie pats her Marie Antoinette costume, which is mostly egg salad–free.

"I don't think we have time to start training a gang of biting cats," I say. "And they won't allow pets in school anyway. We need to beat them at their own game, and I have an idea." Everyone around me leans in closer. "We need to win Spirit Week. We started it. We're ending it as Spirit Week victors. That's how we get even."

"But Spirit Week is canceled," complains Finn, a bit too loudly.

We all put our fingers to our lips. "Ssshhh!"

Mrs. Greeley moves slightly. Her mouth opens a bit wider. A speck of drool falls from her lips and onto the table, which is gross, but she continues to breathe steadily, sleeping.

The group leans in even closer. "It's not canceled unless we say it's canceled," I say. "Tomorrow is Pajamas Day, whether Principal Klein says so or not."

"Will Team Blue dress up, too?" asks Sarah.

"It's all been arranged. Tell everyone. Pajamas Day is tomorrow, and we will win."

Everyone nods, and then the doors to the cafeteria bang open. We turn and stare at Aisha, who hurries into the room. I hadn't noticed her missing. Her lips tremble. "Elvis!" she shrieks.

"Keep your voice down," Sarah orders in an urgent whisper. Somehow, Mrs. Greeley doesn't awaken. She still breathes soundly as I turn back to Aisha. "What's going on with our class turtle?"

"I went to feed him," she says. "B-But h-he's missing," she stammers.

"How could he be missing?" I ask. Elvis doesn't do very much. You could watch him in his terrarium for hours, and he won't move more than an inch. Still, he's our class pet, and class pets are important. I even fed him once, and I think he smiled at me.

"I don't know what happened," says Aisha, her lips quivering. "Maybe he escaped? He could have dashed out of his home when no one was looking or something." She sniffs. "He's probably really scared, too." Her voice trembles with worry.

"That turtle is way too slow to escape," says Sarah. "He isn't some magic disappearing turtle."

"I don't like turtles," says Grace. Sarah nods in agreement.

"Elvis is really sweet and would never hurt anyone," says Aisha, frowning. Her eyes water up.

"He's the nicest turtle I know," I say. Of course, he's the only turtle I know. "And our class pet. The Team Red pet. He's important."

There's only one thing that could have happened. Sarah and Grace and Finn and I all say the same thing at the exact same time: "Team Blue."

I knew Team Blue would stop at nothing, but I never imagined they could sink as low as swiping Elvis. I think of George. He's good at organizing stuff, and he probably organized stealing our turtle.

Organized crime, that's what this is.

"But Elvis would never hurt anyone. Why steal him?" asks Aisha, wiping her nose and sniffling.

"Because everyone on Team Blue is mean and horrible," says Sarah.

"And stinky and vicious," agrees Grace.

"We have to hurt them where it hurts the most," whispers Sarah. Our entire table, about a dozen kids, has gathered around us to listen. Meanwhile, Mrs. Greeley snores away. "We need to fight fire with fire."

"We win Spirit Week," I insist. "And Pajamas Day."

Sarah shakes her head. "We'll do that, sure. But they snatch our pet, we'll snatch theirs, too."

"You mean Soda?" asks Grace. "The guinea pig?"

"Actually, she's a hamster," says Aisha. "We'll do a class pet hostage exchange."

Everyone seems to like the plan, because we all nod our heads and smile, even Sarah and Grace, and they hardly ever smile, although their smiles look more evil than happy.

"We need a small team," I say. "A super spy team to nab it." I look around my group and pick the sneakiest people to go. "Sarah, Grace, and me. We'll go." I glance at our teacher. She is breathing heavy and her eyelids twitch as if she's in some deep slumber. "We should leave now, before Mrs. Greeley wakes up. If she discovers us gone, we'll all be in even bigger trouble than we are already."

"I'm going, too," insists Aisha, her face a firm wall of determination. She still wears her Jackie Joyner-Kersee track outfit, so she looks fast. "If we find Elvis, he'll be scared if I'm not there."

"He's a turtle," says Sarah, rolling her eyes. "He has a brain the size of a grain of rice."

"You can come," I say. Grace and Sarah throw me a dirty look, but Aisha is good with animals, and she could be helpful.

I grab my backpack and sling it over my shoulder. "We can keep Soda in here. She just better not poop." I don't know how big hamster poop is, but I don't want it in my backpack.

We slowly creep toward the door. We only take about five steps, and I know we're supposed to be quiet but sometimes I can't help but bounce when I'm excited, and I bump into a table. The legs screech and someone's book falls over. We freeze.

Mrs. Greeley fidgets. Her mouth closes and we stay motionless, not daring to move a muscle. But then her sleepy breathing begins again. We wait a few seconds, and when our teacher remains motionless, we continue sneaking out. A few moments later, after no more table bumps, we're in the hallway and ready to steal a hamster.

25

GEORGE

Brian has Elvis in a shoebox.

I don't know how and when he and Seth managed to sneak out of detention to grab him. I don't know what they're going to do with him, but I don't like it one bit.

Sliming was bad enough. Egg salad was even worse. But they've gone way, way over the line. I gave Principal Klein my word that we wouldn't do anything else wrong.

We all sit on the gym floor. It stinks in here and I'm sweating, and I rub my hands with hand sanitizer. Then I stand up and take a deep breath.

I avoided Brian and Seth all afternoon. I don't know what they are planning to do with Elvis, and I don't want to be locked in a closet again, but I need to speak up. I'll tell Brian and Seth they have to return Elvis immediately. It's my job as team captain, even if I don't have a team anymore to captain.

"Sit down, George!" orders my teacher, Mr. Foley. He sits in a chair he brought into the gym, and is facing all of us. "You're supposed to be writing an essay on good sportsmanship."

I sit back down, secretly relieved. I'll talk to Brian and Seth later.

I start to write, but I don't just write one page about good sportsmanship, I write four pages. I write about how winning doesn't mean anything if you don't win honestly, but playing honestly isn't enough. You also have to make sure everyone else plays honestly, too. I feel guilty the entire time I write.

I wasn't expelled today, but maybe I should have been.

Brian and Seth smirk. They don't even attempt to write an essay, and instead spend their time passing notes. I hear faint sounds from Brian's shoebox.

I will say something to them right after detention, I promise myself.

26
LILLY

We move quietly in the hallway, staying close to the walls as we walk. You can never be too careful when you're sneaking into school, because Principal Klein or any other teacher could be lurking anywhere.

As we walk, Aisha's gym sneakers squeak. She removes her shoes.

Grace's shoes squawk. She also removes her shoes.

We approach the fifth-grade hallway. We haven't seen anyone, but I peer around the corner just to make sure. It looks clear, so I wave the group to hurry along with me, and I open the hallway doors.

Aisha rushes ahead of us and straight to Mrs. Rosenbloom's room, where she throws the door open and it hits against the wall with a loud BANG!

She turns back around. "Sorry, guys." Fortunately, I don't think anyone heard the bang except us. We all follow her inside the room.

The lights in the room are turned off, but sunlight streams in through the cracks of the blinds covering the windows. The only sound is a slight chattering from Soda's cage, which sits on a table next to the window.

Soda licks from a water bottle that's almost empty.

"Let me do it," says Aisha. She gently lifts the top of the cage, places it quietly on the table, and then scoops up the hamster. Soda squeaks and sort of chirps. I'm glad Aisha is with us, because I know she'll be extra gentle with Soda.

As Aisha nestles Soda in her hands, the hamster looks around, eyeing all of us, and then fixes her stare on me, just me, as if she knows I'm the team captain.

I stare back. "Blame Team Blue," I tell Soda. "This isn't my fault."

I unzip my backpack, which is empty except for my pencil bag, and Aisha places Soda gently inside. She keeps part of my bag unzipped so Soda can breathe.

Soda immediately begins scratching the sides of my pack as if trying to crawl out. I don't think she likes being inside my dark bag. Meanwhile, the wall clock ticks above the door. We've been gone too long, and I feel panic gurgling in my stomach. "We should head back before Mrs. Greeley wakes up." The others nod.

I open the door, look both ways down the hall, and we file out. Soon we are tiptoeing back down the hall to the cafeteria.

Sarah grabs my backpack. "I'll take that. I want to bring the rodent home tonight and make some improvements to it."

"What are you talking about?" I gasp. "I thought we were going to exchange Soda for Elvis."

"Tomorrow," says Sarah. "I have plans for Soda."

"What sort of plans?" I ask. My insides start to hurt with worry. What if we're thrown in jail for hamster stealing? Maybe Sarah likes to eat hamsters. Or maybe she wants to sell Soda to a hamster farm somewhere, although I'm not sure if a hamster farm is actually a *thing*.

None of this is Soda's fault. To be honest, I think she's cute. I asked my parents for a hamster a few years ago, but they didn't let me get one.

"Don't worry," says Sarah, who must sense my worrying. "I won't harm it. Our night together will be fabulicious."

As we walk back to the cafeteria, my stomach twists and turns because I don't know what Sarah has planned. Whatever it is, I doubt Soda will like it one bit. I start to reach for my backpack, to grab it from Sarah, but then I think of Team Blue, and how they stole Elvis.

I watch Sarah walk ahead with my backpack. If George can mastermind a little organized crime, then so can we. Soda might be an innocent bystander, but there is nothing innocent about Team Blue.

27
GEORGE

After detention, I'm standing outside school, near Brian and Seth. They wait for a parent to pick them up. I live close enough to walk, but not everyone does, and buses left an hour ago.

Here is finally my chance to speak up. I walk up to them. I stand in front of them.

"Guys, I wanted to talk about Elvis."

Brian glares at me. "What about him?" He holds the shoebox in front of him.

"I don't think taking a turtle is, well, nice."

Seth laughs. "What does being nice have to do with anything?"

"Maybe Simon needs to lock you in a closet again," says Brian, glaring at me.

I gulp, because I don't want to be locked in a closet, even if I can organize one well. "We just wrote essays on good sportsmanship."

"I didn't," says Brian. "I drew pictures of rocket ships."

"Me too," says Seth.

Team Red files out of school, dozens of kids joining us on the sidewalk. Lilly, Aisha, and Grace stomp up to us. I smile at Lilly, but she doesn't return it. They all stare daggers at us.

"We know you have Elvis," says Lilly.

Brian returns her glare. "Maybe we do, maybe we don't." Lilly stares at the shoebox in Brian's hands, and I can hear the turtle moving inside it, rubbing against the cardboard. "I bought new shoes," says Brian, as if explaining why he might be carefully holding a shoebox that's making noise. "They're running shoes," he adds.

"We have Soda," says Grace.

Kyle, who is standing near us, immediately joins our circle. Kyle usually takes care of Soda, so I think the mention of the class pet's name startles him. "Soda? What about Soda?" he asks loudly.

"We have her," says Lilly.

Kyle's eyes widen. "Where?"

"Somewhere safe, don't worry," says Lilly. "We just need Elvis back first."

Kyle looks at us, puzzled. "Elvis?"

"Don't play dumb with us," Lilly warns, her voice clipped and short. "We'll swap."

"Tomorrow morning, meet us behind the school," says Grace.

"With Elvis," adds Aisha.

"Or you'll never see your precious guinea pig again," says Grace, sneering.

"Actually, she's a hamster," says Kyle.

"Whatever it is, if you want to see it again, you'll meet us tomorrow," Lilly growls.

"You just better hope our turtle is okay," Aisha says.

"You better hope our hamster is okay," Kyle retorts.

All this plotting and stealing makes my head hurt. "Guys, this is all getting out of hand."

Lilly looks at me, eyes narrowed. "You started it."

I put my hands up. "I didn't do anything . . ."

"Save it," she says. "I don't want to hear any more of your excuses."

"I swear . . . ," I begin, but Lilly is already walking away, with Aisha and Grace next to her.

"We have to get Soda back," says Kyle, his voice shaking.

"We will," I assure him. "Um, right, guys?" I ask Brian and Seth.

Brian nods. "Elvis will be there tomorrow. Don't worry. I just might, you know, make him a little more attractive. Turtle green is such a boring color."

I fix them with a steely gaze. I need to stop this, as I promised myself. I open my mouth and start to say, "You can't . . ."

But my voice is drowned out by a loud car honk. A large sedan pulls up to the curb, repeatedly honking. Brian and Seth dash toward it and get in. The car door is only open a moment, but I can hear a loud voice of someone's dad yelling at them before it closes.

I haven't moved, my mouth still open. I spoke up, but not nearly enough. I need to act like our team leader. I'll say something to Brian and Seth tomorrow. Maybe.

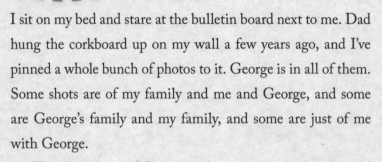

28
LILLY

I sit on my bed and stare at the bulletin board next to me. Dad hung the corkboard up on my wall a few years ago, and I've pinned a whole bunch of photos to it. George is in all of them. Some shots are of my family and me and George, and some are George's family and my family, and some are just of me with George.

There's a photo of George and me at a baseball game, and one at the beach house our families rented for a week. I have a photo of George at my birthday party last year. There were about twenty kids at my party, but the only photo I have is with George. There's a photo of me getting on the bus for camp last summer. George didn't go, but instead of shots from camp pinned to the bulletin board I have a single photo of me posing with George near the front of the bus, waving good-bye.

When I was in camp I wrote to George every day. I only

wrote to my parents twice, and that's because the counselors made us write to our parents twice.

I can't believe I wasted so many great times hanging out with a good-for-nothing cheat and turtle stealer like George.

Still, I miss him.

He's too serious much of the time, but not always. He laughs at my jokes, even when they aren't funny. He is always interested in what I'm talking about, even if what I'm talking about isn't very interesting. And he let me win at tic-tac-toe 228 times in a row, even if he pretended he was trying his hardest.

My wrist feels empty without our friendship bracelet on it. I know I only wore it for a few days, but I expected to wear it forever.

I think about Soda, too. I wonder if she's okay. I can't imagine Sarah would hurt her, but I just don't know what to think about anything anymore except that losing is for losers.

And right now, I feel like I'm losing.

I don't feel good about anything I've done this week. I've cheated. I've stolen. The things I've done during Spirit Week have been even worse than promising a unicorn ride for Francine Pepper's cookie sales.

Maybe, sometimes, being a winner or a loser has nothing to do with winning or losing.

"How's it going, champ?" Dad asks. He and Mom stand in my doorway, smiling, holding hands.

They hold hands a lot. I like that about them.

"Everything's fine," I say, but I don't say it with a lot of happiness I guess, because Dad sort of frowns.

"We still need to talk about school today," Mom says. "Your costume was covered in eggs. You stayed after school to serve detention. When you were named team captain we didn't think . . ."

"I know, okay?" I interrupt. Mom looks angry, and I bite my lip. "It's been a bad week. But everything is fine now."

Mom arches her eyebrows.

"Some kids got carried away and some egg salad got spilled, but I didn't do anything," I continue. "It was just some dumb kids. I don't want to talk about it."

"You're going to have to talk about it at some point," says Mom, frowning.

Dad sighs. "We also came up here with some good news. This Friday, instead of eating in, we're going out to a restaurant with George and his family. Any suggestions where we go?"

I always choose the Japanese steakhouse near us. I love how the chefs clang their knives together and make silly jokes while they throw pieces of vegetables at us. We're supposed to catch the veggies in our mouths, but George always misses.

They pour oil in an onion and it steams up like a train. It's awesomesauce.

But today I just shake my head. "I don't care where we eat."

"You always care where we eat," says Dad.

"Well, I don't care now, all right?" I say, trying to keep the irritation from my voice, but I know it's spilling out.

Dad walks into my room and stands next to my bed, looking down at me. "We haven't seen George in a few days. Is everything okay with you guys?"

"You should ask him," I answer, and now I'm even more annoyed and I can hear it in my voice.

"Mrs. Martinez says she hasn't seen you at their house in a few days, either," adds Mom, also walking into my room, and standing next to Dad.

I take a deep breath. So I haven't been seen with George for a few days. You'd think the world was coming to an end. "I'm okay, okay? Everything is great. Everyone is great. I'm just not hanging out with George anymore. Is it against the law not to hang out with George?" My voice gets louder and louder as I talk, and I don't want it to get louder and louder. It just does. When I stop talking the room is eerily silent. Both Mom and Dad's mouths are open.

"Well, all right, then," Mom says, and I know I've totally overreacted to their questions. But she acts as if I'm committing some horrible crime just because George and I aren't doing things together.

I sigh, extra loudly for effect. "I'm sorry. Everything is perfect," I lie. "Can't you guys see I'm busy?"

"When we came in you were just sitting on your bed staring at the wall," says Mom.

"Well, to me that's busy."

"Listen, young lady . . . ," Mom begins, her voice rising, but Dad puts his hand on her shoulder, which calms her.

"We will talk later, when we're all in a better mood," says Dad, and he speaks in this sort of quiet, understanding voice that is more irritating than if he just spoke normally.

He and Mom leave, and they are holding hands again, which I guess is nice since they are best friends. But I don't have a best friend anymore, so looking at their hands suddenly bothers me. I turn away and look at the bulletin board again. It takes all my strength not to jump up and rip all of the photos with George off the board, right then and there.

29

GEORGE

School starts soon but I stand behind it, in my pajamas. I'm with Kyle, Brian, and Seth in a secluded spot hidden from the street, where no one can see us. The only other things that move are the grass and trees from a slow, cool breeze. The school-building shadows cover us.

I hate what I'm wearing. All of my pajamas were in my dirty clothes hamper except for one pair, which I've only worn once before today. Mom apologized. She meant to do the wash last night.

So now I'm stuck wearing these pj's, the ones Grandma Katie bought for me as a birthday present last year. They are pink. Grandma said they're lavender, but they look pink to me. Brian and Seth both already informed me that boys don't wear pink. I didn't bother trying to explain it was lavender.

Still, it's Pajamas Day, even though it's not really, and I'm the team captain, so I need to wear jammies.

Brian, Seth, and Kyle all wear pajamas, too. But they all wear normal-colored ones.

A back door opens. We turn. Lilly exits the building with Soda cradled in her hands. Sarah, Grace, and Aisha walk behind her.

Lilly wears mismatched pajamas. Her shirt is striped and green. Her pants are red and plaid. I've seen her wear the same outfit at her house, when I've come over to watch TV after dinner. I never really thought about it before, but now I think it looks sort of ridiculous.

Those nights seem a lifetime ago.

"Nice outfit," I say, shaking my head because I don't really mean it.

"At least I'm not wearing pink," Lilly answers, rolling her eyes.

Sarah and Grace stand behind her, glaring with huge frowns. But Aisha is all smiles. "Elvis!" she shouts with glee.

The turtle sits in my hands. I have one hand under him and my other hand covers his shell. Egg salad smells worse than turtle, but not a whole lot worse. I can't wait to exchange our pets and wash my hands. I'll need to soak them in water and soap for an hour or I'll never get rid of the turtle germs.

Kyle, standing next to me, tries to get a look at Soda. "She better be okay," he huffs.

"Relax," says Lilly. "She's never been better."

"She even has a new fashion accessory," adds Sarah. Lilly uncuffs her hands to reveal Soda, who has a giant red stripe across her back with the fur propped high like a Mohawk. "Quite an improvement, don't you think?"

I can feel Kyle shaking with anger. "If you've harmed her . . ."

"Oh, relax," says Grace. "It'll wash out."

"Unfortunately," adds Sarah.

I hold up Elvis, who has withdrawn into his shell. I don't think he likes it here, outside his terrarium. I remove my top hand.

"What did you do to Elvis?" asks Aisha, her voice high-pitched, angry.

"Gave him a touch-up," says Brian.

He and Seth wrote *Go, Team Blu* on his shell with blue paint.

"We ran out of room," explains Brian, pointing to the word *Blu*. The letters are pretty large.

"How dare you mess up his shell!" Aisha cries out, taking a step forward.

"It'll wash off. But how dare you give Soda a Mohawk racing stripe!" Kyle retorts, taking a step forward.

Sarah steps forward, too. Her eyes burn, and for a moment I think everyone is going to start fighting.

"Stop it!" I yell, and I surprise myself by yelling. "All of you."

Kyle steps back, as does Aisha. Sarah doesn't move, but she doesn't come closer, either.

"We're here to swap," I say. "Let's just get this over with."

"But her fur . . . ," Kyle blares.

"His shell . . . ," Aisha blurts.

"George is right. Let's just do this," grumbles Lilly. She seems as disinterested in fighting as I do.

I hand Elvis to Aisha, and Lilly hands Soda to Kyle. As we do this, our shoulders slightly graze. "I'm sorry, it wasn't my idea . . . ," I say.

Lilly sniffs. It's a sniff of scorn. "You always have an excuse, don't you?"

I bristle at this and I want to say something back that's just as mean, but I can't think of anything. I just feel guilty for everything.

"We'll see you in the gym for Pajamas Day," says Sarah.

"I hear the winning team gets a new house. A house just for Elvis to live in," Aisha adds. She hugs the turtle like it's her best friend. But I notice Elvis hasn't come out of his shell. I think he just wants to go back into his home.

"You mean, a new house for Soda to live in." Kyle hugs the squirming hamster, but she doesn't seem happy out here, either.

"Whatever that prize is, we're going to win it," says Grace.

I don't say a word, but I know Principal Klein is not giving anyone a prize. I think we'll be lucky if he doesn't expel the entire grade, since he has already canceled Spirit Week and we're all wearing pajamas, anyway.

I sigh. Why did I agree to this?

Kyle, Brian, Seth, and I walk away, Soda cradled safely in Kyle's arms. "Poor girl," he says to her in a soothing voice. "But don't worry, no not today. For you, we'll win Pajamas Day," he says in a sort of rap.

I don't say anything. I just want this week to end. Why did I ever raise my hand to be the team captain?

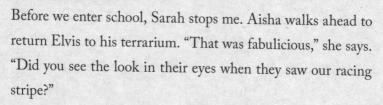

30
LILLY

Before we enter school, Sarah stops me. Aisha walks ahead to return Elvis to his terrarium. "That was fabulicious," she says. "Did you see the look in their eyes when they saw our racing stripe?"

"Yeah, but Elvis is painted blue," I point out.

Sarah nods. "We'll get revenge for that, too."

I get that sinking feeling in my stomach again. "Do we have to keep getting revenge?" I ask. "I mean, we swiped their pet. We're dressed in pajamas. What else is there?"

Sarah squints. "Losing is for losers. And letting the other team get away with painting our turtle—well, that's for losers."

"I know but . . ."

Sarah keeps her eyes narrowed. "Maybe you don't have what it takes. I thought you could hang out with us after school sometime, but maybe Grace and I were wrong about you. Don't you want to win Spirit Week?"

"Sure, but there is no more Spirit Week. I mean, not really, right?"

Sarah shakes her head in disgust at me. "Grace even said she was going to let you ride her horse."

Sarah marches ahead, joining Grace, who is waiting for her up by the school entrance. I walk slowly by myself thinking of Francine Pepper, pretend horseback riding, and feeling like I've lost already.

As I head back into the school, which is now filling up with the rest of the students, I'm amazed at how many fifth graders are wearing pajamas. I guess word spread quickly, and I didn't text anyone about it, either. It's like we're having one big sleepover. Some outfits are sort of funny, like Daisy's bunny pajamas, with ears and everything. I see Maggie, who's back in school with her arm in a cast, and even she wears pj's. I'm not sure how she heard about our plan, but her crimson Harvard sleepwear is exactly what I'd expect the brainiest girl in our grade to wear.

I consider gathering all my notes and handing them to Maggie. She can be our team captain now! Then I remember it's too late. Spirit Week is over, despite our wearing pajamas.

"Hey, Pinky," says Luke with a laugh, and I cringe. He's wiggling around as always, and I'm jealous of his normal, not-strange-at-all green flannel pajamas. They have a thousand wrinkles over them, though, and I wonder if he thrashes around all night, just like he seems to be jittery all day. "Looks like Pajamas Day is actually happening, huh? Do you think we're going to get in trouble? I mean, after the egg-salad disaster and everything?"

I feel a lump in my throat. "I don't know."

Luke hops in place for a moment. "I hope not. I mean, we're just wearing pajamas. There's no school rule about wearing pajamas, right? So, anyway, how are we voting for a winner? Our team better do the counting. Because I don't trust anyone on Team Red to count right."

"I haven't thought about the judging," I admit.

"Well, you better. You're team captain, right?"

I nod, although I hate those words.

As we all walk toward the gym, Harrison, who is in Lilly's class, stumbles in front of me. At first I think it's because of his big fuzzy slippers. But I hear a laugh and realize Brian and Seth are behind me. They shove kids on Team Red, because that's the sort of thing they do.

Brian shoves Pedro, who knocks into Jessie. She's wearing a yellow onesie spotted with pictures of cats. "Watch it," she says. To Brian she adds, "Or I'll sic my cats on you." She almost seems feline herself, with her cat-eye glasses and angry snarl. Brian laughs, but I don't think you want to mess with Jessie and her cats.

"Give it a rest, you guys are being pests," rhymes Kyle, and Brian and Seth stop shoving people. Kyle's the only guy who can ever talk sense into those two. He no longer carries Soda, who is probably resting comfortably back in her cage.

Soon, we enter the sweltering, sock-smelling gym. My lavender pj's are itchy and warm, and I'm already feeling sticky. My team gathers on the far side of the gym. As I join them, kids stick out their palms to exchange high fives with me. "This was a great idea," says Toby.

"It wasn't my idea," I say.

"You know, I can still give you free fashion advice if you want," says Samantha, tapping me on the back and eyeing my pajamas. I blush, and my face probably turns the same shade as my outfit.

The bell rings and that means classes are starting. I wonder what our teachers will think when no one shows up. We're definitely getting expelled. My heart beats faster. I just want to get this over with. I walk to the middle of the gym, and so does Lilly. We meet at the centerline of the basketball court.

"Clearly, Team Red wins Pajamas Day," she says.

I scratch my head, looking at her side and mine again. "What are you talking about?"

"Every kid on Team Red is wearing pajamas."

"So is everyone on Team Blue," I point out.

"Even them?" She points to Danny and Jasmine, twins, who stand near the bleachers wearing blue jeans and T-shirts. I didn't notice them earlier.

"That's what they wear to bed," I say, which I'm guessing isn't true. I point to her side of the court. "And what about them?"

Clearly, Taylor and Olivia are not dressed in pajamas. They both wear dresses and matching green sweaters.

Lilly frowns. "Those are fancy pajamas."

"So here you are." The booming voice of Principal Klein interrupts our meeting. He's hovering in the doorway with Mrs. Rosenbloom by his side. His frown is as long as his face. He stands with his arms crossed, face red. "What is going on here?"

"We're dressed for Pajamas Day," says Adam, who stands near the door. I cringe, because that's not something you should say to a principal who has clearly forbidden Pajamas Day. I think Adam realizes this, because he immediately steps back and hides behind the much-taller Kyle.

"I see," says Principal Klein. The entire gym is quiet. We stare at our principal. I knew we might get in trouble, and I was up half the night worrying about what could happen.

But now, with our principal here, even the worst things I imagined don't seem bad enough.

From the expression on Principal Klein's face, we are in trouble and the trouble is deep, deep, deep. "And who thought this was acceptable?"

No one says a word.

"Spirit Week was canceled because of continued poor sportsmanship, trickery, and tomfoolery," he says, his voice getting louder with each word until it echoes off the walls and bleachers. "It was canceled because, in all my years as principal, I have never seen a fifth grade act with as much malice as all of you." He looks around the room. "And yet here you are, wearing pajamas, skipping class to assemble anyway." His voice rises both in loudness and pitch. "Whose idea was this?"

I look at Lilly, because the answer clearly is *Lilly*. This was all her thinking. She's the one who's created all these problems to begin with, too. I almost shout out, "It was all Lilly's fault," but I hold my tongue, because I don't want to bring attention to myself.

I'll probably be banished from school. And it will all be because of Lilly.

Principal Klein is pacing now. He's not limited to pacing behind his desk in his small office, so he takes long strides back and forth. Kids veer out of his way. "I have never, ever witnessed a more disrespectful group of students. You disrespect the school and me personally. It seems that your serving detention yesterday didn't teach any of you a lesson. So maybe this will—you will all serve detention after school again today."

"But I have baseball practice," complains Seth.

Principal Klein scans the crowd, trying to see who dared speak out, but Seth stands still and seems to shrink just a bit, and our principal doesn't notice him.

There are a few murmurs in the crowd, Seth's outburst seeming to puncture the incredible silence from the kids. Maggie, who stands near me, complains to her friend Lacey that she'll miss her private tutoring classes, and Samantha tells Giovanna she has violin lessons. But most of us are still too nervous to say a word.

I wonder what Lilly is thinking as she stands there, frowning, hitting her fist against her leg. Does she blame herself, like she should? Does she blame me?

Principal Klein talks with Mrs. Rosenbloom now. She nods, and we're all waiting and wondering what they are talking about, but everyone is too nervous to say anything, and after maybe a minute, Principal Klein turns back to us. "Ms. Bryce runs an after-school tutoring program for some of the younger kids. In addition to your detention, you will all attend the program and help instruct the children over the next few weeks. I will create a schedule and share it in a few days. Attendance is mandatory."

Maggie leans over to her friends Lacey and Paige. They all wear the same glasses and look sort of like owls. As Maggie talks she moves her one good hand, since the other is still in a cast. "We're so lucky. I wonder if we can volunteer for multiple tutoring days? I bet we can teach some of those kids a lot."

Paige and Lacey nod their heads in eager agreement. But most of the kids in the gym groan.

"Everyone back to class," says our principal. "Now."

As Lilly and I step forward, our eyes meet. "This is all your fault," she whispers in a nasty tone.

I look at her, and I realize that she is right. "I know." Her eyes widen. I don't think she was expecting me to agree with her. I might not have come up with the idea to wear pajamas today, but I'm wearing them. I am a team captain. That means I'm the leader, only I haven't been doing much leading. I spent time organizing, and that's important, but leading is more than that. It's about doing the right thing, setting an example, and keeping your teammates in check.

I did none of that. I could have spoken up a bunch of times, but I was silent or spoke so softly no one could hear me. And even when I wasn't silent or locked in a closet, did I do everything I could? Did I demand my teammates behave, or was I just afraid?

Doing nothing is sometimes just as bad as doing something. Sometimes it's even worse.

"Lilly, it's your fault, too," I add.

"But I didn't start—"

"Does it really matter who started what?" I can tell she is about to yell at me, so I quickly add, "We both could have stopped this. But I was too scared and you were too competitive." Lilly opens her mouth to argue, but I continue. "You are, Lilly. That's usually okay. But we were both thinking of that stupid prize."

"I heard everyone on the winning team was going to win five thousand dollars," she adds.

"I don't know what we were supposed to win," I said. "But can you put a price on cheating? On doing bad things?" I squeeze her arm. "Or on our friendship?"

With that last word, Lilly's head slumps, and when she looks back up, she smiles. It's a sad sort of smile, but her eyes wrinkle, so I know it's a genuine smile. "Our friendship is worth more than five thousand dollars, or a truck of ice-cream cones, or whatever the prize was. I'm sorry about everything."

"Me too."

Her smile broadens. She no longer looks sad. She looks relieved. "I guess I got carried away, and I know you didn't do any of that stuff, but it made it easier to plot things if I convinced myself you were behind them. And Sarah and Grace said . . . Well, never mind them. But how are we going to make things right?"

"You mean between us?" I ask.

She shakes her head. "That won't be too hard, I think. But we're the team captains. We need to make things right for everyone. But how?"

"I wish I knew." I look down at the ground. I don't think there is any way to fix what we've done, other than serve our punishment.

As we head out of the gym, all our classmates walk with their heads as bowed as mine.

32
LILLY

We stream out of the gym under the watchful glare of Principal Klein. I slink down so he doesn't notice me. I really, really don't want to be noticed right now.

George walks ahead of me, but I can't get his words out of my head because I know he is right, just like I've known every moment of every day that he's not organizing crime or anything. He's not against me. He's my best friend.

Our entire grade walks down the hall without saying much of anything. I think we all feel bad about wearing pajamas today.

While I walk, Seth bumps me on the shoulder. "Sorry," mutters the Team Blue bully. But he's not sorry. That was definitely an on-purpose bump. I guess not everyone feels as bad about things as others.

But Team Blue shouldn't hate me. I didn't force them to wear their pj's. They could have worn whatever they wanted and let us win the contest.

They all chose to be just as guilty as me.

I approach my locker. "I can't believe we get detention and community service and no special prize," moans Grace, her teeth bared like a wolf.

"It's the worst," agrees Sarah as she removes books from her locker. The inside of her door is still tinged with slime stain from the other day, as is mine. "I heard the winner was going on a cruise to the Bahamas."

"And it's all Team Blue's fault," barks Finn.

"We're going to make them sorry," adds Pete. Both Finn and Pete wear dark blue flannel pajamas with our school name across the front: Liberty Falls Elementary.

"We sure are," agrees Sarah.

Anger oozes from all of them, but I no longer share their hatred. I just feel bad for playing any part in the mischief. If I could rewind the week, I would. Too bad life doesn't come with a remote control.

"Guys, relax," I say. I keep my voice calm. "I'm not saying Team Blue isn't guilty, but so are we, okay? We put pudding in half the balloons, you know."

"That was different," says Sarah.

"How?" I ask.

"That was revenge because they filled our lockers with slime," says Grace.

"Which was revenge for Lilly deliberately ruining George's twin outfit," adds Aisha.

"That was an accident," I insist.

"Right, I know," says Aisha, but Sarah and Grace just laugh because they don't believe me at all.

"Look, it doesn't matter," I say, and I'm thinking of George the entire time I talk. "We've all made mistakes. We might as well own up to them. And maybe if we do . . ." My voice trails off, as an idea slowly forms in my head.

George and I talked about making things right. Maybe there's a way. The idea is a bit murky, but something about it feels like it could work.

"Maybe if we do what?" asks Finn.

The idea grows and it forms into a solid block of promise, kind of like when clay hardens in the oven. It's not a great idea, but it's not a terrible one, either. "It starts by taking responsibility for everything we did. It starts with an apology to Principal Klein." I eye my teammates. "And maybe even an apology to Team Blue."

"Never!" yells Sarah, spit flying from her mouth.

"I don't apologize," says Grace. "Apologies are for losers."

"And so is losing," adds Sarah.

"Hear me out," I say. Grace and Sarah seethe, but they wait for me to finish. "Principal Klein is angry because he says we're bad sports."

"Team Blue started it," insists Grace.

"Look," I continue, and I'm nodding my head as I talk because this idea of mine feels more right the more I think it. "It doesn't matter who started what. If we apologize, maybe, just maybe, Principal Klein will change his mind about canceling the week. It's a long shot, sure. But if we show him we can play fair, maybe we can convince him that the best way to learn how to be good sports is to be good sports."

"And then we can destroy Team Blue?" asks Grace, her eyes menacing slits.

"Well, first things first," I say.

Sarah shakes her head. "Apologizing won't change anything."

"I have to agree," says Aisha. "An apology sounds nice and all, but Principal Klein was pretty mad. I don't think an apology is enough for him to change his mind."

"You're right," I say, nodding my head. "That's just the first part. But I know something that might help, a secret something. We're going to need Team Blue's help with this, but if we work together, just maybe . . ."

"Work with Team Blue? Are you nuts?" says Grace.

"I've been looking forward to Field Day for years, and it was supposed to be tomorrow," I say. "Maybe it still can be? I don't know. I'm just saying that it's worth trying. But we need everyone's help if we want to win that prize."

"Do you think the prize could be horseback-riding lessons?" asks Finn.

"You never know," says Grace. Finn grins broadly.

We huddle together as I share my plan. I can tell from the vigorous nods of their heads that they agree it's worth trying, although Sarah grumbles the entire time.

But we have to try something.

33
GEORGE

The entire day is a haze. Our parents were called and we all served detention again. This time we were told to write a one-page report on why it's important to listen to your teachers and follow rules in school. I wrote a five-page report because I couldn't get all I had to say on only one page.

I wrote about how keeping silent is just as wrong as doing bad things. I wrote about how it's not easy to stand up for what you believe in, but if no one ever stood up for things, then good things might never happen. I wrote about how pens should be kept in penholders on desks.

That last part didn't make much sense, but I kept thinking of Principal Klein's desk and it just sort of flowed into the essay. I also wrote about the importance of hand sanitizer.

As soon as I leave detention, I look for Lilly. I'm determined to walk home with her today. I want to forget this week ever happened. Part of me is happy we're not finishing Spirit Week. I hated being team captain.

But I don't have to look for Lilly because she finds me. "George. Good. We need to talk."

"We can talk while we walk home," I say, smiling.

Lilly doesn't return my grin. She speaks with urgency. "Look, I think we can still finish Spirit Week."

I shake my head. "It's over, Lilly. I'm sorry."

"I think we can save it. Well, maybe we can save it."

"You're crazy. You heard Principal Klein," I argue. "You're just going to get us in more trouble."

She takes hold of my arm, and I shake it loose from her grip. She's obviously lost her own grip on reality. "Just hear me out. I need your help."

"You didn't need my help to make a mess of everything." I immediately wish I hadn't said that, and I bite my lip. I thought I had sort of forgiven Lilly, but maybe not entirely. Lilly frowns. "Sorry. I didn't mean that."

"That's okay. Maybe I deserve it." She looks me in the eye, and I know all is forgiven. "But it's in the past. You can organize things better than me. You're better at making lists and stuff."

"I know. So?"

"So we need to act quickly. If we want Field Day tomorrow, we can't mess around. We're going to need a lot of people to help. And both teams will need to work together."

Lilly tells me her plan and when she's done, I have to admit, it's not the worst plan ever. It's a bit scattered and messy, sort of like Lilly, but with some proper planning and organization, it could come together.

I mean, it probably won't work, but maybe it's worth attempting. It would mean I'm still our team captain, at least for tonight, and maybe tomorrow. But I guess I can handle it for one more day.

"Okay, I'm in," I say, and Lilly beams. I haven't seen her smile in days, not a big, broad smile like this one, and it warms me.

I text my mom that I'm going to Lilly's. But instead of leaving, we get too excited, and Lilly and I just plop down on the sidewalk in front of the school. I grab my notebook and we get to work. I have a lot of note taking to do. We'll need to get most of the grade involved. But if we all work together, who knows? Even if it doesn't work, it just feels right to be on the same team as Lilly.

Lilly smiles and bounces next to me as we make plans, and it seems like everything that has come between us just sort of fades away.

I only wish we had been on the same team all week.

34
LILLY

George and I stand in front of Mrs. Frank's desk on Friday morning. I fold my hands behind my back and smile. School hasn't started yet, and the school secretary has a giant mug of coffee steaming in front of her. "He's a busy man," she says to us.

"We just need to show him something," I say, making my smile more of a friendly grin since it's always a good idea to smile at people if you want them to do things for you.

"Please?" adds George.

Grown-ups love it when you say *please*. You can get them to do just about anything with that word, especially when you throw in the smile. Mrs. Frank sighs, puts down her coffee, and stands up. She turns the knob to Principal Klein's office door and then disappears inside without even knocking.

That's sort of rude, but I guess when you're the school secretary you don't have to knock.

"Do you really think this will work?" George asks.

"I have no idea."

The door opens and Mrs. Frank steps out. Principal Klein walks out with her, still looking angry from the day before. He folds his arms in front of him. "Hello, George and Lilly," he says, his voice clipped. "What can I help you with?"

"We wanted to show you something," I say, my smile plastered on my face.

"In the gym," says George.

"School starts soon," says Principal Klein, his arms still folded, his voice still short and growling a bit. "Shouldn't you be getting to class?"

"Please? It will only take a few minutes," George says. He smiles. I smile.

Principal Klein scrunches his brows. He looks back into his office. A half-eaten bagel sits on his desk.

"It's important," I add.

Principal Klein blows out a heavy sigh. "What is it?"

"We have to show you," I say.

Principal Klein sighs again, and this sigh is louder than the first one.

"Please?" I ask, using the magic word.

"Tell my morning appointment I might be a few minutes late," our principal says to Mrs. Frank.

"That's been canceled. I forgot to update you, sir," says Mrs. Frank.

Our principal frowns and then follows us out of the office.

Kids are rushing down the halls to get to their lockers or to class, but as soon as anyone sees Principal Klein, he or she slows down. It's pretty funny, actually. Four third graders skid to a halt and start walking in slow motion. A large gang of second graders who are sprinting immediately freeze, as if turned to ice. Principal Klein frowns at each and every one of them.

But we don't pass any fifth graders. They are waiting in the gym.

As we walk, with Principal Klein right behind us, I can't believe we did it. George and I share a smile. If they had assigned teams like they were supposed to assign them, with George's class and my class together, maybe none of these problems would have happened. So, in a way, this entire week is our principal's fault.

But I'm not about to tell him *that*.

"We're almost there," George says to Principal Klein.

"Humph," he replies with a frown.

As we near the gym, a loud buzz fills the hallway from the kids inside.

"How many people are in there?" asks Principal Klein.

"The entire fifth grade, I think," I answer.

I push open the doors. The lights are off so we step inside a darkened gym.

35

GEORGE

A light flickers on, a spotlight aimed at the middle of the gym floor. Kyle stands in front of the microphone. Behind him are Finn and Jai, who start to beatbox.

Ryan spins next to them performing some sort of twirling dance. She's a dancer, and she really wanted to do an interpretive spinning dance. I suppose it adds to the spirit of the assembly we've created.

Kyle starts to rap, the beatboxing behind him driving the rhythm.

Principal Klein, welcome to the show.
Our grade's got plenty to show you, yo!
No, we haven't gone mad or berserk.
But you can do tons with lots of teamwork.
We got together, Team Red and Team Blue,
To prove what working together can do.

A switch is flicked and the gym is bathed in dancing green lights. The entire gym has been transformed. Giovanna and Samantha were in charge of the decorations, and they filled the room with streamers and lined the walls with dozens of posters with words like TEAMWORK, SPORTSMANSHIP, and FAIR PLAY. I don't know how they got it all done in one night.

Meanwhile, most of the class sits on the bleachers, clapping along to the rap while Kyle continues.

Like the auditorium—filled with slop.
So some of us came early—with a mop.

He points to a group of fifth graders who hold up their mops. I looked in the auditorium this morning, and I don't think it has ever been so clean.

Kyle continues.

But that's not all, no that's just the start.
Everyone here did a little part.
Like Bjorn, in charge of technology,
And Maggie, who wrote an apology.

Bjorn hits a button on his cell phone, and the room, which had been basked in green light, is now awash in red. He really is good at computer stuff. He rigged all the lights together.

Kyle points to Maggie, who stands off to the side, holding a piece of paper in front of her. She clears her throat. "Dear Principal Klein, we are sorry for acting so poorly. We have learned a valuable lesson about teamwork and fair play. We let our competitive spirit get the best of us, and we realize we were wrong. Please accept our sincere apology. P.S. We can't wait to help out with Ms. Bryce's after-school tutoring program, and can I have some extra sessions, please?"

She runs over to our principal and hands him the note, which has been signed by everyone in our grade.

Our principal accepts the page, his mouth agape. I don't know what he was expecting when he came to the gym, but it wasn't this.

Finn and Jai begin beatboxing again, and Kyle continues his rap.

Great lessons and values, we've learned a ton—
About sportsmanship and playing for fun.
But we've brought you more than my rap ballad.
We've also brought some homemade egg salad.

Toby runs over to our principal with a bowl of egg salad his mom made last night. Toby said his mom makes a really good egg salad. "Here you go. I know it's your favorite," says Toby, and then runs off.

We worked together to bring you this song,
And show you that our grade can get along.
So now we're one team, and those are the facts,
Now let's take a break for Luke on the sax.

Kyle points to Luke, who's dressed in his Charlie Parker costume from Historical Figure Day. He is in front of a microphone, and he starts blowing his horn and moving his fingers at crazy speeds while he taps his toes and wiggles his legs. The entire room fills with the honks and beeps from his instrument.

I find myself tapping my foot and snapping my fingers. Luke ends with a manic flourish and then points back to Kyle.

Thanks for your time—soon the school bell will ring,
But we need to show you one final thing.
It's big and awesome and can't be ignored,
But the world's best principal deserves an award.

Bjorn hits his phone, and the gym fills with a dark purple light, all except for one bright spotlight. It shines on a large trophy, a three-foot statue of Principal Klein made of modeling clay and the words *World's Greatest Principal* etched on the bottom.

Our principal's jaw drops open in surprise. I think that's a good thing.

Of all the things we did to make this Principal Klein presentation, the trophy was the most impressive. I've always liked making figurines, but I've never made anything this big. Aisha and Giovanna both helped me last night.

I'm not sure if our trophy looks like Principal Klein, but it's a large guy wearing an orange cardigan sweater, so there is no doubt who it's supposed to be.

Principal Klein stares at it, his eyes practically bugging out of his head. He walks toward the clay trophy, slowly at first and then picking up speed. George and I follow him. He stands next to it, staring, as if he's afraid to touch it, as if it might all disappear if he takes even a small step closer.

"I can't believe you were able to make that in one night," George whispers to me.

"It was a very late night, but I heard Principal Klein say that he'd never won a trophy before," I whisper back. "He always wanted one. I hoped to make it taller, but we ran out of modeling clay."

When I look at Principal Klein, I don't know if our plan is going to work or not. He just stares and stares at the trophy. He doesn't seem happy, but he doesn't look angry, either.

The gym is eerily silent except for a couple of coughs.

Finally, Principal Klein reaches his hand out and his fingers gently rub against the clay. They leave a small indent, because the clay isn't completely dry. He pulls his hand back.

He turns to us and sweeps his arms across the room. "You did all of this together?" We nod. "And you made this? For me?"

I nod, beaming.

"This is the . . . ," he begins, his voice starting to rise. "This is the . . ." His voice is louder, and I can't keep from fidgeting I'm so nervous. "This is the nicest thing anyone has ever done for me."

I had been holding my breath for a long time, and I can hold my breath for a very long time, but I let it out in a big sigh of relief. So does George. So do about half the kids in the bleachers. I hear a WOOSH of air around us.

"This will look marvelous in the trophy case," says Principal Klein, his voice choking. "Well, maybe it won't fit in one." He looks disappointed for a moment, but then adds, "But I'll put it somewhere." He circles the sculpture. George and I step back to give him room. He turns to George and me. "How did you guys put this together so quickly?"

"Both of our teams worked together," says George. "It's amazing what you can do with a little teamwork." He flashes me a smile, and I return it.

"I'm sure if you gave us another chance, we could show you we've learned all about teamwork," I say to Principal Klein. "And playing fairly. And for fun."

"Then you've learned a valuable lesson," says Principal Klein. "One that can help you throughout your life, and not just today." He looks at us and then at the rest of the grade. Everyone has now gathered in a big circle with me, George, our principal, and the trophy in the middle. We're all smiles.

Then, in his loud, booming voice, our principal adds, "Yes, you all have learned a great lesson. Good for you. Thank you for this wonderful gift." He wipes his nose. "I'm proud to announce that we will have Field Day this afternoon, as planned."

I bounce on my feet and cheer. The entire gymnasium cheers, and I bet we're so loud that every class in the building can hear us. Principal Klein raises his hands, motioning us to quiet down, but it takes a few moments before we do. A couple of lone yelps of happiness ring out, and then we are silent again. "But you have to show me you've truly learned your lesson. Any hint of shenanigans and Field Day will be canceled immediately. Understand?"

"What about the special prize?" someone yells. I can't see who it is. I think it sounded like Sarah.

"If there's a Field Day, there will be a prize," says Principal Klein, and this gets as loud and long a cheer as did his earlier announcement. "But for now, school is about to start and you all need to get to class."

George and I exchange grins. It's a relief to know that we saved Spirit Week. But I feel even better knowing that we saved it together.

37

GEORGE

Instead of listening to Mr. Foley during class, I spend the morning working on today's schedule. Field Day is full of events, and you need the right people assigned to the right games if you want to win.

Everyone talks about what games we'll play this afternoon. There is a lot of whispering in class and Mr. Foley keeps ordering kids to be quiet, but even he seems excited about Field Day.

Brian and Seth whisper and pass notes constantly, often while giggling. That worries me.

I try to put them out of my mind and concentrate on my schedule.

Most events need somewhere between ten and twelve kids from each team, and every kid is supposed to be assigned to participate in at least two events. It's a little tricky figuring it all out, and knowing where some kids will be great, and where other kids might not do great, but won't be too awful. For example, there's Avery, who is nice and all, but sort of clumsy. She wouldn't be the best person to choose for the Egg Race. And Maggie has her broken arm, so I wouldn't want her balancing cups of water.

But other kids would be perfect for those events. Other games need different skills, like the Tug-of-War, which is all about strength. With guys like Brian, Seth, and Kyle on my team, we should dominate Tug-of-War. That's the final event of the day and worth double points.

"This will be fun," says Luke after the bell rings and we head outside for the start of Field Day. He's changed out of his Charlie Parker costume from this morning, and instead wears a yellow T-shirt and jeans. I blink twice. The jeans are glittery with rainbow patches on the pockets.

"Are those from the Lost and Found?" I ask.

Luke shakes his head. "No, I had my mom make them. I thought they were kind of cool when you wore them the other day." He blushes. "Do I look goofy?"

"You look great," I say.

"Field Day is going to be fantastic," Brian says. He walks with Seth on the other side of me. "I mean, we've been planning stuff for days, you know? I just can't believe it's back on."

"Um, what do you mean 'planning stuff'?" I ask. Brian chuckles. "We have to play fair," I remind him. "We all promised."

"Sure," he answers with a wink. "Fair play. No worries."

I eye him suspiciously. He wears a smirk, and you should never trust a smirk.

"I hear nothing can stop us from winning," adds Toby, behind me. He's grinning, too.

"What's going on?" I demand. "What did you hear?" I cry out to Toby as he rushes past me.

Brian puts his finger to his mouth as a group of Team Red kids near us, also heading outside.

As I walk down the hall, my heart races. I should have known those guys would try to ruin everything. I need to scream at them that we need to play fair. We just performed a whole rap song about it!

But the hall is crowded, and Brian and Seth are now way ahead of me, exiting the school doors.

I also remember being locked in the storage pantry and how big Brian and Seth are, and so I take a deep breath. Maybe I can avoid talking to them. Maybe things aren't as bad as I think.

But then again, they could be even worse.

38
LILLY

Field Day always starts with hot dogs, and hot dogs are awesomesauce. I grab one from the lunch cart and then I stand in the fields behind the school with the rest of my team. It's surprisingly hot today! It almost feels as steamy outside as it usually does inside the gym. There is no breeze, and a breeze can make all the difference. A few portable fans sit on tables, but those are mostly for the parent volunteers, who stand next to the fans at their Field Day stations.

I'm amazed they got so many volunteers with such last-second notice, although Zachary said he heard that Mrs. Frank forgot to call parents to tell them today was canceled.

Everyone on my team wears a bright red Team Red shirt. They were handed out as soon as we walked outside. Big orange cones mark off courses, and ribbons and tape stretch across starting and finish lines for relay races. Spray paint outlines a football field. A lot of time and effort was spent preparing for all of this.

I guess Mrs. Frank forgot to tell the volunteers not to prepare the fields yesterday, either. Mrs. Frank seems to forget stuff sometimes.

There is a lot of equipment and gear, like a stack of Hula-Hoops sitting on a table and a long cord of rope lying on the ground for Tug-of-War. Ms. Bryce stands by a giant table covered in buckets that are filled with old, weird clothes.

I hold a small notepad, where I've scribbled down the participants for our first couple of events. I was supposed to do that this morning, but then I started thinking about what restaurant we should eat at tonight, because Mom and Dad said I could pick and I completely forgot to pick one, so I didn't have time to finish my Field Day assignments.

I squint while I read what I wrote. Is that Aubrey or Amelia? And which Alex did I want to participate in that event? There are two Alexes on my team. I can't read my writing very well. I should have been paying more attention to my writing and less to dinner.

But there is nothing wrong with being spontaneous.

I'll just figure out the rest of it as we go along. I'm sure George has mapped out some complicated schedule for his team, but you don't win by scheduling. You win by doing.

I look up at a giant board that marks each team's total points and will be updated after every event. My team is winning ten points to five for the week. That's not a very big lead. We won

Twin Day, but then both teams were awarded five points for the pudding fight because they called it a tie, Historical Figure Day was ruined, and Pajamas Day didn't count, either. Whoever wins the most events today will win Spirit Week and get the mystery prize.

The last I heard, the special prize is a waffle iron. I guess that prize would be sort of nice, but I don't think that rumor is true because winning a waffle iron would be weird.

George waves at me. He stands with his team, all wearing their royal-blue Team Blue T-shirts. He mouths, "Good luck!"

"You too!" I mouth back, and I mean it. I still want to win more than ever, but I want us both to play well. Winning only really counts when both teams try their hardest. Otherwise, it's not really winning at all.

George starts jogging over to me, and he's holding something in his hand. I meet him halfway across the field, and I can't see exactly what he carries until he's almost next to me.

"New friendship bracelets." He hands me one made from green, yellow, and blue twisted strings. The other bracelet is already around his wrist. "I made them last night. I should never have tossed the old one, but I'll never take this one off."

"Ever?"

His smile vanishes. "If it gets dirty, I might need to take it off to clean it, and I don't want to get hand sanitizer on it, and it could break someday maybe, but otherwise, never."

George keeps his smile off. He stiffens his neck and puts on his Mr. Serious expression. He frowns. "But look, we need to talk. We've got trouble. Kids are planning stuff. There's Brian and Seth, of course. But maybe Toby and other kids, too. I'm not sure, but I think my team has planned all sorts of sabotage today."

"Like what?"

"I don't know. But I think it's bad. Real bad."

"We'll just have to keep an eye out," I say. "We gave our word we would play fair. Maybe you've got it all wrong."

"I don't think so, but I hope you're right. I'll snoop around some more and see if I can figure it out."

"I'll do the same."

I jog back to rejoin my team, but my stomach is already feeling queasy. I smile at Amelia. "Ready to play fair?" I ask. But she just returns my smile with a frown.

"We're going to win," says Sarah to Grace.

Grace nods. "They won't be expecting anything."

"How could they?" asks Sarah. She snickers.

I tap them both on the shoulder. "Expecting what?"

Grace shrugs and Sarah laughs.

"We need to play honestly," I plead. "We gave our word."

Finn walks up to us and says to Grace, "We're all set."

"What's all set?" I ask.

They ignore me.

"You have to stop whatever you're planning!" I urge.

"It's too late now," says Grace.

"Tell me what you've done," I demand.

"So you can blab to your friend George?" asks Sarah, shaking her head and rolling her eyes. "Don't think we haven't noticed. You're either on Team Red or Team Blue. But you look awfully blue to me."

"I'm team captain."

"Not a very good one," says Sarah. "And you can forget about any sleepovers or horseback rides."

I wheel away, my head swimming. Sarah, Grace, and Finn huddle together, whispering. Then Zachary joins their huddle, and then Koko. I don't know how many people are involved or what horrible things have been planned, but it seems like a lot of potential planners and a lot of potential plans.

"What's happening?" I ask Aisha. She stands by herself, stretching her arms and legs.

"As if you don't know," she says.

"I don't!"

Aisha shakes her head and walks away from me. "I thought you were against cheating, too."

"I am!" She continues walking away and I want to scream. I want to pull out my hair, I'm so frustrated, but no one will even look at me.

Across the field, George jogs toward me again, and I run to meet him. I need to warn him about the pranks we're going to pull, even if I have no idea what they are. "What did you learn?" I ask.

"Nothing. No one will say a word to me."

"Same over here," I admit. "We've planned things, things that are maybe even worse than what your team has planned. But no one will tell me what."

"We've got to stop it," says George. "I'm too young to get kicked out of school."

"I don't want to win by cheating. Not anymore. No matter what the prize is."

"Then we've got to be ready for anything," warns George. "Because it's up to you and me to make sure both teams play fair or we're going to be in big, big trouble."

"The biggest," I agree. "As team captains we'll be blamed for everything."

I look down at my new friendship bracelet. I'll keep my word and play fair, but I'm not sure if I can get the rest of the team to do the same, even with George's help.

39
GEORGE

Large fans are positioned near many of the events, but they don't cool you off unless you're standing directly next to one. The teachers and adult volunteers have already taken all the good fan-standing spots. My jeans stick to my legs and sweat covers my forehead.

I squirt hand sanitizer on my palms, using up the final drips of my small bottle. This day will be sweaty and dirty. I groan.

The first event of the day is the Egg Race. One person from each team puts the handle of a spoon in his or her mouth, places an egg on the spoon, and then races across the field while trying to balance the egg.

Then he or she passes the egg to the next member of the team, who has his or her own plastic spoon.

I had to choose ten racers for the event. I didn't pick fast runners, but steady ones. If you drop the egg, you have to go back to the beginning, so you need balanced racers who aren't all twitchy like Luke. Luke would be a horrible egg runner.

Each of my Team Blue egg racers run in a circle, balancing a math book on his or her head. I read that beauty pageant contestants do that, to help with posture. Mario keeps dropping his books, so I replace him with Gavin at the last minute. Gavin seems more balanced, although maybe he just has a flatter head so books don't fall as easily.

My racers jog over to start the event. So do the Team Red racers. The rest of us crowd around the sidelines to cheer them on. Lilly has picked tall, fast kids, but a wobbly fast kid won't win a race for you. I feel good about our chances.

I wish I stood next to one of those portable fans, but I'm sweating from more than the heat. I'm sweating from nerves because I'm worried about what might be planned by my team, and that could be nearly anything. There's a buzz of excitement for the first event to begin, and that makes my nervous butterflies flap harder.

I look down at my notebook, clutched tightly in my grip. I've jotted down all of today's events with my lists of who will be participating in what. But I've also scribbled down ways I think each event can be sabotaged.

Principal Klein smiles broadly while the contestants gather around him and a parent volunteer explains the rules, rules that I'm sure someone will be breaking.

I read the list of potential hazards I wrote in my notebook.

Someone could be planning on:

- Untying everyone's shoelaces (so they trip).
- Digging a giant hole for the racers to fall into.
- Unloading a cage of chickens to attack our team.
  (Maybe chickens can identify which eggs belonged to
  them, and they will seek revenge?)
- Throwing erasers at our runners to knock eggs off
  spoons. (I hear Brian and Seth like to play a game called
  Eraser Wars.)
- Replacing our eggs with eggs that are about to hatch.
  We can't carry a live chicken on a spoon!

But honestly, my list doesn't seem particularly helpful.

"Stop staring at that page," orders Lilly. She pushes my notebook away from my face.

"Hey! You could wrinkle the paper." I brush my notepad to smooth it out. "How else are we going to figure out what's happening?"

"Scan the crowd. Use your eyes. Watch everything. Hopefully we'll spot the plan."

"If there is a plan."

Lilly frowns. "Oh, there's a plan. Somewhere."

I nod. I know she's right, and I mentally check the things off my list. Everyone's shoelaces are tied, no one is holding erasers, and I would notice a cage of angry chickens or a giant hole in the ground.

Half the racers line up behind the starting line, which is also the finish line. The other racers jog to the opposite side of the field, for egg swapping. Bella will be the first racer for my team: she's short and a gymnast, and I figure gymnasts have great balance. Team Red's first racer is Wesley. He's a good athlete, but tall. He'll lose time if he needs to bend over and pick up a fallen egg. My racers are all short, so the egg has less distance to drop.

While Principal Klein finishes explaining the rules to the racers, Simon carries two baskets of eggs. He puts one down by Team Red, and the other by our team.

He wipes his hands on his legs, rubbing off some sort of goop—egg yolk, I think.

My stomach is in knots.

Lilly taps me on the shoulder and points to Seth and Brian. They are smiling and whispering, and smiling and whispering is never a great combination when it comes to them.

I can't hear what they are saying from this far away, though. Lilly said I should keep my eyes out. Maybe I should also keep my ears out.

I sneak closer to them, gliding past Maya and Trinity, skipping past Daisy and leaning in behind Kim.

"The yolk's on them," says Brian with a giggle.

Seth nods. "All over them."

"You crack me up."

"Eggs-actly." Then they laugh loudly, too loudly.

I strain to listen to more of their conversation, but other people are talking and I can't hear anything else unless I move even closer, but then my eavesdropping would be way too obvious. At the starting line, Bella and Wesley hold their egg-filled spoons in their hands. They stand, crouched, ready to run. One of the parent volunteers raises her hand.

Lilly wiggles past a few kids and taps me on the shoulder. "What's going on? Did you hear anything?"

Simon stands behind the racers, grinning.

That's when I put it all together. Brian made a confusing yolk joke. Simon carried the eggs and wiped egg-dripping fingers. "Um, the eggs. They are supposed to be hard-boiled, right?"

Lilly nods. "Of course. Otherwise they would break too easily."

"But what if Team Red's eggs weren't hard-boiled? What if they were replaced with regular eggs, or eggs with small cracks in them already? Just think how easily they would break."

"I don't see how they could switch eggs," says Lilly. "You'd need to be the one preparing the eggs."

"Simon, Brian's brother, works in the cafeteria. And he's up to no good."

Lilly's eyes open wide, and she doesn't wait to ask me more questions. Instead, she's all legs and sprinting. She pushes past kids, but there are many in the way. She nudges Avery, nearly trips over Allie, and elbows Elias.

"We'll begin on the count of three," says Principal Klein.

I'm not sure if Lilly is going to make it to the starting line before the event begins, and if she does—I don't know what she plans to do. All I do know is that if our principal discovers that eggs have been switched, Field Day could be canceled before it even begins, and our entire class will probably serve detention for years.

As a team captain, Principal Klein could keep me in detention until high school. Maybe I'll never be allowed into high school, let alone middle school next year.

"One . . . ," says Principal Klein.

The contestants put their spoons in their mouths.

"Two . . . ," says Principal Klein.

Bella and Wesley balance their egg on their spoons.

"Thr . . . ,"

Before Principal Klein can finish even saying *three*, Lilly bludgeons past Derek and Mario.

I see the entire disaster clearly.

Lilly is running too fast.

Her foot hits Mario's left leg.

She topples forward, both of her legs leaving the ground as if she's trying to fly. But she can't fly. Instead, she rams directly into Gerardo, who stands behind Wesley, next in line to race for Team Red.

Gerardo stumbles forward and smacks into Wesley's back. Wesley lurches forward, his mouth opening and the spoon toppling out. Wesley falls to the ground. The egg splatters, cracking into pieces. Wesley falls right next to the shattered egg.

But Lilly is like a freight train that can't stop. She continues falling forward, past the stumbling Gerardo, hitting Pete, and flopping to the ground, where her shoulder collides with the entire basket of Team Red eggs.

The basket falls over. Lilly's entire body continues skidding forward, still moving, and sliding directly on top of the eggs.

". . . ree," continues Principal Klein. But no one moves.

Wesley is on the ground. Gerardo is on the ground. But worst of all is Lilly. She lies, face-first, on top of about two dozen broken eggs.

Lilly rolls over onto her back, eggshells sticking to her hair and yolk smeared across her face. She looks up at

Principal Klein, who stands only a few feet away. "Um, sorry?" she mumbles. "I sort of tripped."

As Lilly stands up, egg dripping from nearly every inch of her, Bella remains at the starting line, standing. She removes her spoon from her mouth. "Should I still run?" she asks Principal Klein.

If she does, we'll win. Team Red doesn't have any eggs left.

But Principal Klein doesn't answer. He looks at Lilly. "Are you okay?"

Lilly nods. "Just a little messy."

"I see." Our principal looks at the ground again and at the egg calamity that covers it. He looks at the parent volunteers. He looks at Lilly. "I thought these were supposed to be hard-boiled." He frowns, scanning the ground and the baskets. "If this was sabotage, we'll have to cancel . . ."

"I was in charge of the eggs, sir," says Simon, stepping up. "But no one told me they were supposed to be hard-boiled." I know he's lying, and the frown he throws at Lilly drips with wickedness and spite.

"Oh my," says our principal. "I'm not sure how things got so confused. Yes, they are always hard-boiled."

"I wish I had known that, sir," says Simon. "Taking care of the eggs is an important job, you know."

"Of course it is," says our principal, nodding vigorously. "No one can blame you. But we don't have enough eggs to go forward with this event, I'm afraid." He looks again at the parents, and then at the egg mess. He shakes his head. "We'll just call this one a tie."

Lilly is a walking egg disaster, but she releases a long sigh of relief. So do I. Lilly looks happy, even with eggshells sticking to her eyebrows.

I think our team would have won this event if we hadn't decided to cheat, but I'd rather tie than win dishonestly.

One event is over, but I know that this is only the beginning. Who knows what other trouble is planned and whether we'll be able to stop it. It will just take one mishap to ruin everything, and I don't think I can plan on Lilly tripping over someone's leg before every event.

"Anyone have a spare towel?" asks Principal Klein, and a parent volunteer hands Lilly a rag to wipe off the yolk. But I have a terrible feeling that things are only going to get messier.

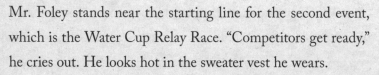

40

LILLY

Mr. Foley stands near the starting line for the second event, which is the Water Cup Relay Race. "Competitors get ready," he cries out. He looks hot in the sweater vest he wears.

Maybe he should call it a sweating vest. His hair, a thick curly ball of black, wilts in the heat.

George's squad gathers around him for instructions. I can't hear what George says to them, but he looks prepared, as if he has a plan all figured out, but of course George would have everything arranged.

My team stands around me. I picked everyone for this event alphabetically by first name. It was the fastest way to choose participants, since I didn't have much time between events, but now I regret not picking my teams more carefully.

"What's the plan?" asks Alex.

"Um, run as fast as you can?" I suggest with a helpless smile. Other than Alex and Aisha, who are both tall and fast,

I think my team might be in trouble during this event. "You'll be okay running?" I ask Charlie. When I assigned him to this race, I forgot he had a broken leg.

"I can hop," Charlie boasts, handing me his crutches and then hopping three times to show me.

His hopping might have been more impressive if his arms didn't fly up every time he moved. I'm not sure how he's going to keep his water cup balanced. But I don't have the heart to take him off the race team. He seems excited to participate.

Each team member has to balance a cup of water on a tray, sort of like a waiter, and then race to a bucket at the far end of the field. Then he or she dumps the water into the bucket, runs back and hands the tray and cup to the next racer, who fills the cup with water and runs back across the field. The race goes back and forth and back.

Whoever fills their bucket with water first, wins. So balancing your water cup is a pretty important part of the race.

"I'm ready, too," says Brianna firmly. Then she hiccups. My eyes widen. That's also going to be a problem. "It's"—hiccup—"fine. I can"—hiccup—"do this," she insists. Then she sucks in a big gulp of air and holds her breath.

Brianna sometimes has hiccupping issues.

"I'll need to walk very slowly," says Colby. "I don't want to twist my ankle. I have a big match tomorrow, and Dad told me to be careful." Colby is a really good golfer, so I guess it makes sense that she needs to be careful, but it will take a miracle for us to win this event.

Finn stands near me. He's not in this race, but he leans over and says, "Don't worry. We can't lose."

"What do you mean?" I ask, but Finn walks away muttering something about Grace and horseback riding.

I start to chase after him, but Mr. Foley is already in position to start the event. I'm just going to have to keep my eyes as wide-open as they can possibly be open. Something's going to happen, and I only wish I knew what.

"Your team looks good," says George, but I know he's just being polite. "Choosing Charlie and his broken leg was an interesting choice."

"He can hop," I say, biting my lip. "But never mind that. Do you see any sabotage planned?" I'm eager to change the subject from Charlie's hopping skills.

"No," admits George, looking this way and that way. "But maybe nothing will happen during this race. At least there aren't any eggs involved."

I shake my head and pick an eggshell out of my hair. "I'm pretty sure Finn did something, or he will do something. Grace has him wrapped around her finger."

The first racers, Bjorn for Team Blue and Aubrey for my team, stand with their trays at the starting line, their water cups full. Two large buckets sit on chairs at the far side of the field.

"Are you ready?" asks Mr. Foley as sweat pours down his face. He stands in front of one of the fans, but it's not blowing enough air to keep water from dripping off his head. "On your mark."

I still don't see anything wrong anywhere. "What's going to happen?" I ask George.

George looks down at his clipboard. "Maybe it will rain and water will fill all the buckets so it'll be a tie?"

I shake my head. There's not a cloud in the sky.

"Get set," Mr. Foley announces.

George looks down at his clipboard. "I thought someone might replace one of the buckets with a thimble so only a tiny amount of water would fill it." George frowns and lowers his list. "And that was my best idea."

"You're not very good at planning trouble." I squeeze his arm. "But that's one of the things I like about you."

"Go!" yells Mr. Foley.

Bjorn and Aubrey are off. Bjorn walks slowly, careful not to spill his water, but Aubrey shoots ahead of him. She's fast and we take a quick lead. "You don't have a chance of winning if your team goes that slow," I warn George.

"Slow and steady wins the race," he replies.

Sure enough, Aubrey stumbles and her water cup flies off her tray. Bjorn from Team Blue walks as slowly as Elvis the turtle, but he's not spilling a drop. As he trudges forward, Aubrey scrambles to her feet and rushes back to the starting line to refill her water cup.

By the time Aubrey finishes filling her cup and dumping it into the bucket, we're behind. Brianna is up next. She's speedy and catching up, but then she hiccups. It's one very, very loud hiccup. Her tray wobbles and the cup teeters.

She swallows some air, smiles, and then runs forward. Her hiccups seem to have hiccupped themselves out after only one. I breathe a deep sigh of relief. She's neck and neck with Lizzie from Team Blue.

"Go, Lizzie!" yells Adam from the sidelines. Lizzie turns her head and smiles. She raises her hand to wave to Adam, forgetting she's holding a tray.

Her cup of water topples over and drenches her pants.

"Pay attention!" cries George, pulling on his hair.

Lizzie rushes back to the starting line to pour water back into her cup while Brianna speeds ahead. My teammates roar their approval.

"All right, Bri!" I shout.

Soon, we're a lap ahead of Team Blue, which is awesome-sauce, but now it is Charlie's turn to run. I can barely watch. He left his crutches on the ground, but his water cup falls every time he hops. Hop, spill. Hop, spill. I really should have replaced him in this race.

After Charlie hops back to refill his cup for the fourth time, he gets down on his knees and crawls forward with his cup and tray. He isn't hopping and spilling all his water out, but he's also creeping like a snail, and our lead vanishes.

Both teams cheer wildly as Charlie finally dumps out his cup and hops back to the start, his arms flailing to keep himself steady. He's actually surprisingly fast when he hops. But we're now two or three cup pours behind.

I don't know how full our water bucket is, but it can't be nearly as full as the Team Blue bucket. I slip past my clapping and hollering teammates and walk to the end of the field for a closer look at the buckets.

I stand on my tiptoes to get a good look. Our bucket is more than half full, but Team Blue's bucket is almost empty.

I blink and stare at it again. I must be seeing things.

Nope. Their bucket is almost empty, but that's impossible.

Or it should be impossible. When I look closely, moving a little farther down the line so I see the back of the buckets, I spy a small but steady stream of water flowing from the bottom of Team Blue's bucket.

A hole. Someone jabbed a hole in the bottom of the blue plastic bucket.

Surprisingly, no one else has seemed to notice. There are no volunteers standing back here to look, probably because there are no fans over here and the volunteers want to keep cool. But one of the parents looks like she's getting ready to check the buckets.

When she gets here, she will see exactly what I see. This will be a disaster. Instead of prizes we'll get lectures, detention, and who knows what else? Nothing good, that's for sure.

Don't my teammates understand they need to play fair?

Finn and Pete whisper to each other near the starting line. Sarah and Grace share a laugh.

No, they don't know how to play fair.

But I gave my word we wouldn't cheat. I need to fill Team Blue's bucket with water before the scheme is discovered.

If only it would rain! As I look around for anything, something, I don't know what, my eyes rest near the supply shed at the back of the school. That's where the ground crew's industrial-strength sprinklers are lined up.

Sprinklers mean water. Industrial-strength sprinklers mean a whole lot of water. That would be even better than rain.

While racers run with trays and water, I sneak over to the sprinklers. The crowds cheer. Even Principal Klein claps.

Then a parent volunteer starts walking down the line, toward the buckets. She is almost at the end.

But I have already reached the sprinklers.

I take a deep breath.

I reach down and twist the sprinkler spigot.

And then I run.

The hose bulges with water.

I'm already back near the pack of kids when the water erupts.

The sprinkler shoots water directly into the line of kids watching the race, a downpour of industrial-strength wetness. The sprinkler clicks and twists, spreading water from left to right, across our entire group. CLICK, CLICK, CLICK, it says. The water soaks me, but since I'm already sort of covered in egg, the water feels good, cleaning me.

But the water spray doesn't stop. The sprinkler head continues to click and rotate. The spray soaks the racers waiting to run, and then the teachers and parents.

The stream of water reaches across the field and cleanly knocks our bucket off its chair, and then the Team Blue bucket gets walloped by water, too.

Then the water stops.

A rainbow forms across the sunny sky from the mist of sprinkler water clinging to the air. Behind it, a red-faced and very angry Principal Klein stands next to the water faucets.

41

GEORGE

I'm convinced Field Day will be canceled. Principal Klein huddles with the fifth-grade teachers, and they each wear deep frowns. All the teachers' clothes are soggy, all the parent volunteers' clothes are soggy, and all the students' clothes are soggy. Only Mrs. Rosenbloom seems to have completely avoided the sprinkler shower, and Principal Klein just has water soaking the bottom of his gray slacks.

Since it's so hot today, many kids seem sort of glad they got doused. Lilly stands next to me, a sparkle in her eyes. The water has washed off most of the egg yolk that still clung to her. She's holding something behind her back, but I can't see what it is. We are close enough to the teachers that we can hear their conversation, or at least we can hear Principal Klein. His loud voice is impossible to miss. We could probably hear him even if we stood clear across the field. "We have to cancel," he says.

Lilly and I scoot a little closer so we're at the very lip of the circle of students all waiting for the conversation to end.

Luke stands next to me. "What do you think they'll do?" he asks, his legs wiggling and his arms twitching.

I put my finger to my lips. I want to listen.

"It's not the students' fault the sprinklers turned on," says Mrs. Crawford.

"Are you sure?" asks Principal Klein, his voice rising.

"Of course I'm sure. Who would do such a thing?" asks Mrs. Rosenbloom.

"I agree," adds Mrs. Greeley. "There has been plenty of poor sportsmanship this week. But those sprinklers ruined both teams' chances to win, not just one."

"But what about the Egg Race?" Principal Klein asks. "That was spoiled, too."

"An accident, plain and simple," says Mrs. Rosenbloom.

Mrs. Greeley nods. "Lilly is a bit of a klutz."

I giggle and Lilly elbows me in the ribs. "Well, you are," I say. "I mean, just a little."

She frowns.

"And you can't blame her for the eggs being made wrong," Mrs. Greeley adds.

"Did any of us see a student turn on the sprinklers?" asks Mrs. Crawford in a clipped, scholarly tone.

All the teachers shake their heads, including our principal.

Lilly lets out a loud sigh and grins. She must have turned on those sprinklers, and I'm sure she must have had a good reason. I assume she stopped some sabotage that I didn't see. I give her arm a gentle squeeze. "Nice job," I whisper.

"Most of those sprinklers are set on timers," adds Mrs. Crawford, as the teachers remain gathered together. "Maybe one just got knocked off its correct time. That sort of thing happens all the time."

This comment gets the other teachers nodding their heads in agreement.

"I can't recall that sort of thing ever happening," counters Principal Klein. "But I suppose it could. And we can't punish the students because someone may have done something. Not if we don't know for sure."

Mrs. Crawford pats the principal's hand, like a parent might do with an upset baby. "I once set the timer for a meat loaf wrong, and it cooked for four hours instead of forty minutes. We had to order a pizza since the meat loaf just wasn't edible."

"A shame," says Mrs. Greeley. "I love meat loaf."

"I think we can all agree that meat loaf is a tasty dinner," says Principal Klein. "But we are not making meat loaf here. Any more suspicious acts will force an immediate cancellation of Field Day."

"Of course," agrees Mrs. Rosenbloom.

"Absolutely," says Mrs. Greeley.

"And worse," says Principal Klein. "A deliberate action to ruin today would result in catastrophic punishments for the kids."

Lilly grips my arm. "What do you think they would do?"

"I don't know and I don't want to find out. There have to be more things planned today, but we can't go around ruining every event. The teachers will be onto us."

"We need to be smarter," agrees Lilly.

I hold up my notebook and tap the page. The water stream soaked my back, but I was able to cradle my notebook so it's mostly dry. "That's why I wrote down all my thoughts. The Hula-Hoop contest is next. What if someone replaced round Hula-Hoops with square ones?"

Lilly laughs. "I think everyone would notice that."

"I guess so." I cross that off my list.

"Besides, I've already figured out what was planned for the Hula-Hoop contest," says Lilly with a grin.

"What? When?"

"When everyone was drying themselves off, Zane dropped this." She shows me what she has been holding behind her back. It's a small and very soggy paper bag. She lifts out a box of pepper from inside it. "The Hula-Hoop contest is right next to one of those big fans. I think Zane, or someone, was going to put the pepper over the fan and make the contestants sneeze. You can't hula-hoop while sneezing."

"But wouldn't that just make everyone sneeze and everyone lose?"

"Not if someone on my team was wearing nose plugs." She holds the bag upside down, and a dozen small spongy plugs fall to the ground.

I bend down and pick one up. "So the entire team was in on it?"

"I don't know. It just takes one person to win. Grace is one of my Hula-Hoopers, and I wouldn't put it past her to be involved."

I'm relieved the Hula-Hoop contest sabotage has been discovered, but there are plenty of events left and plenty of mischief we need to uncover. It will take a miracle to get through the day.

I check my notepad. "I'll run through my notes for the next few events. I have lots of ideas for what might be planned."

"Just keep your eyes and ears open. And your fingers crossed."

42

LILLY

Eight Team Red and eight Team Blue competitors file into a big spray-painted circle to compete in the Hula-Hoop contest.

George and I personally inspected the Hula-Hoops, just in case someone else planned to ruin this event. None of the hoops are wobbly or falling apart or filled with anything weird, like mustard. I don't know why I thought one might be filled with mustard. I guess I'm as rotten a schemer as George. He thought someone might fill the Hula-Hoops with helium so they would fly away.

Zane frantically runs around, yelling out, "Has anyone seen a paper bag? I had a paper bag!"

I put the bag in a trash can, hidden under random garbage. No one will find it.

Samantha, Giovanna, and five other girls from Team Blue grab hoops, and so does George. I think Samantha and

Giovanna are going to be hard to beat. I saw them practicing earlier, and they looked like longtime Hula-Hoopers. George is good, too. He out-hula-hooped me once, and it still annoys me when I think about it.

My team is not awesomesauce. I picked my team alphabetically again because I had to pick them quickly, so I chose Elle, Esmeralda, Finn, Gerardo, Griffin, Grace, Harrison, and Heaven.

Finn glares at me and mumbles something I can't hear, but it's probably best that I don't. I'm sure it wasn't a very nice mumble. I can tell that he does not want to hula-hoop.

But my team is not without hoop hopes. Heaven and Esmeralda both told me they love hoops, but now that I think of it, they may have been talking about earrings. Harrison said he was great at hoops, but I think he meant basketball.

A few members of my team pick up their hoops to practice. Finn, Harrison, and Heaven can't even make their hoops circle their bodies once without falling to their feet. But I only need one great Hula-Hooper to win. The last one standing wins for his or her team.

I spy Grace talking to Zane, probably about the pepper and plugs. Grace stomps away and toward the event. Even without nose plugs, Grace is my secret weapon. She told me she is a two-time Hula-Hoop contest champion. She won those contests in preschool, but she's our best chance to win.

Mrs. Rosenbloom instructs everyone to get ready. Principal Klein watches from the sidelines, as do all of us kids. Our principal glances at the sprinklers but seems satisfied none are about to accidently start spraying.

Mrs. Rosenbloom pushes a button on a laptop computer that has speakers attached to it. Polka music dances out. She cries, "Start hula-hooping, everyone!"

The spinning begins.

Within seconds, nearly half of my team is out of the competition. Finn, Harrison, Heaven, and Gerardo all fail to complete a single twirl. Finn tromps off, glaring at me the entire time.

But that means half of my team still spins, so we still have a chance. Grace swivels her hips calmly and looks like she could spin all day. Griffin hangs in there by wiggling his arms and moving his legs in an awkward and jerking gyrating motion, but it appears to work. Elle and Esmeralda aren't too bad, either.

But there are plenty of good Team Blue spinners, like George, who swivels calmly. Fortunately for us, two Team Blue players get too close to each other. Their hoops collide and then fall.

The accordion polka music continues. Mrs. Rosenbloom orders everyone to take a step closer together.

As Elle moves in, she walks right into a Team Blue player. They both lose their hoops, and their balance. Elle falls and rolls into the legs of Esmeralda, who rolls into another Team Blue Hula-Hooper, who falls into another Team Blue player.

Samantha deftly steps away to avoid the dominos.

Griffin goes out next, tripping over his own feet but also knocking out Samantha from Team Blue.

Grace is now the only Hula-Hooper left for my team. George and Giovanna remain twirling for Team Blue.

They all look really good. This contest could take a long time until someone wins.

Sarah stands behind me. She talks with Zane. "Why is this still going on?"

"I lost the pepper," complains Zane.

I bite my lip and say nothing.

The music swirls, and Mrs. Rosenbloom orders the three contestants to move closer again. Their hoops are only inches apart as they spin round and round. It's sort of mesmerizing. My teammates yell, "Go, Grace!" and Team Blue's spectators scream out, "Go, Team Blue!"

All three spin and spin.

"Take another step closer," orders Mrs. Rosenbloom.

The three of them take a step closer together, but now they are too close. George's and Giovanna's hoops collide. Giovanna's hoop crashes to her feet, but somehow George keeps his going.

Giovanna picks up her hoop and stomps off.

Now it's down to Grace and George, side-by-side, hips circling, hoops barely missing each other as they twirl around and around. One step closer and this will be over for one of them, or maybe both.

I feel a tap on my shoulder. "It's now or never," says Sarah.

"What do you mean?"

"We can't lose," she hisses. "I found a banana peel next to a trash can." She holds up a black and sort of disgusting peel that is dripping with what might be fruit punch. "I can toss it at George's feet."

She steps forward with the banana, but I jump in front of her.

"Get out of the way," she orders.

I stand firm and cross my arms. "No way. We're going to win fair and square. I've had enough of your plotting. Can't you all just give it a rest already?"

Sarah glares at me. "I knew you weren't on our side."

I don't back down. "I'm on our side, but I'm also on the side of playing fairly."

"You're just a Team Blue lover," Sarah says, and spits as if the taste of Team Blue is on her tongue and it's a sour taste.

"This is just a game," I say. "It's about fair play and . . ."

"This isn't just a game," insists Pete, joining us. "It's about winning a special prize, like a lifetime supply of pillows. At least, that's what I heard."

I want to roll my eyes. Instead, I say to everyone, "Don't you want to win fair and square?"

There's a pause and Sarah shakes her head. "Not really."

Others from our team are listening in. Almost half of my team seems to be surrounding us. This is my moment to show my spirit. This is why I am team captain.

"Whether it's tomorrow or next year or years from now, when you look back at today, don't you want to look back knowing you tried your best?" I ask. I point to Team Blue. "Those are our friends. Sure, they might not be in our class this year, but next year they might be. We go to their birthday parties, just like they go to ours. You don't cheat your friends. You don't plot against classmates just to win pillows, or whatever the special prize is."

"Even if that prize is really, really incredible?" asks Amelia.

"Like a litter of kittens?" asks Jessie.

"Or a giant fortress loaded with gold and zebras?" asks Zachary.

"Yes, even then," I say.

"But I love zebras!" exclaims Taylor. "I look good in stripes."

The circle of Team Red members has grown around me. Not too many kids even watch the Hula-Hoop competition. Some nod their heads, agreeing with me. Others seem uncertain. I can see their brows furrowing as my words sink in.

I have a chance to stop the troublemaking right now. I raise my fist. "Let's win fairly," I declare. "Honestly! For fun and spirit! Who's with me?"

No one says a word.

I pump my fist again. "I said, who's with me?" My teammates smile, and I think many of them are going to shout that they agree.

But then Mrs. Rosenbloom yells out, "And the winner is George and Team Blue!"

George won! I think that's great, but no one else does. Every smile on my team is erased. Sarah glowers at me. "If we lose Spirit Week, it's all because of you."

Everyone trudges off.

Aisha, however, throws me a small smile. She puts her arm across my shoulder. "I thought it was a really good speech." She gives me a gentle squeeze. "Even if no one else thinks so."

"We'll take a short break until the next event," announces Mrs. Rosenbloom. "Who wants a snack?"

Everyone runs off to get in line for food, including Aisha.

I can't get my team as excited about playing fairly as they are about eating a snack. I stand by myself as the grass waves gently around me.

I know we need to play fair. But playing fair seems very, very lonely.

43
GEORGE

After standing in line for a frozen Popsicle, I sit on the grass with my treat. It melts quickly in the heat, so I have to lick the dripping orange juice as fast as I can. A few drops land on my jeans. I rub them, but they leave stains and now my hands are sticky. I wish I had brought more hand sanitizer.

Our principal erases the numbers on the scoreboard. With our Hula-Hoop win, the score for the week is now ten to ten.

"We're all tied up," says Brian. He walks past me with a wink.

"I bet we'll win a lot more before this day is through," adds Seth, walking behind Brian.

They wander to one of the tables where Brian's brother Simon stands, waiting for them. They laugh. They chat. Brian hands Simon a paper bag. More smiles. More laughter.

I stare at them and try to read their lips. But I'm not good at reading lips, and Brian's back is to me, anyway.

I should run over there because whatever they are discussing can't be anything good. I need to stand up to them, like I've promised myself I would. They can't lock me in a supply closet out here either. I am team captain, even if I don't want to be.

Simon walks off, and Brian and Seth sit down to lick their Popsicles. I stand up, ball both my fists, and tell myself, *You can do it, George.* But before I take a step, Lilly sits down next to me. "Where are you going?" she asks. "Hey, we match," she adds, pointing at my orange Popsicle. She eats an orange Popsicle, too.

"Of course we do," I say. I'd rather be sitting with Lilly than standing up to bullies, so I sit back down and lick off a big drop clinging to the bottom of my stick.

I sneak glances over to Brian and Seth. I will talk with them later.

"Nice job winning the Hula-Hoop contest," she says.

"Thanks. Remember when we hula-hooped together once?"

Lilly nods. "I was a bad sport, huh?"

"Well . . . ," I say with a shrug.

"Maybe I'm learning to be a better one." Lilly sticks half the Popsicle into her mouth. When she removes it, her lips are orange and her tongue is orange and half the Popsicle is in her stomach. I really want to grab a napkin and wipe her lips, but my napkin is already a mess from my own dripping juice. "Your Hula-Hoop win doesn't matter anyway. Team Red will win the rest of today's contests. We're winning that prize."

Do her eyes narrow when she says this?

"Relax," she says with a giggle when she notices my eyes widening with worry. "We'll win fairly. At least I hope so. Everyone else seems to know more than me about what's planned, and terrible things are definitely planned."

"Brian and Seth keep snickering, so I know they've got things up their sleeves. They were just talking to Brian's older brother Simon. I think he's a bigger sneak than Brian."

"We'll need to watch them. You know, I heard the mystery prize was a week at the White House. As guests of the president and everything."

"I heard the winner gets a trip to the sun."

Lilly laughs. "Wouldn't you sort of, I don't know, melt?" She wipes her forehead. "I can barely stand the sun out here. I don't think I want to get any closer."

I laugh, too. "Everyone has different ideas of what we'll win, but no one has any clue."

"Koko thinks we all win a llama. Really." She giggles and then takes a big chomp from her Popsicle.

Lilly is almost done with her treat, but I'm still licking mine, carefully catching most of the falling orange before it lands on my fingers.

"Too bad there's not a Popsicle-eating contest," Lilly says. "I think I'd win."

"You just might," I agree with a smile.

I look down at my notebook for hints of what might be planned next. A few Popsicle drops have landed on the paper, and when I rub the spots, the liquid spreads more. I frown and wish I could rewrite the page because I hate paper with stains on it. But I don't have time because the Silly Clothes Race will start in a few minutes.

The first competitor dresses up in a bunch of silly clothes, runs across the field, removes the silly clothes, and hands them to the next racer to wear, who then dresses and runs to the next racer. There are twelve kids from each team.

"So what do you think is planned?" asks Lilly.

I peer at my notebook for hints of plots. As usual, my ideas are not helpful.

- Silly clothes could be replaced with suits of armor that would be too heavy and too hard to wear.
- Rockets could be hidden inside the clothes, so a racer zooms away.

- Giant poisonous snakes could be hidden in clothes and bite everyone.

"So? Any thoughts?" asks Lilly.

I shake my head and rip out the page from my notebook. "I'm a horrible troublemaker."

Lilly smiles. "I know." She gnaws a final bite from her Popsicle and jumps to her feet. "I'm going to look around."

She walks away to snoop, and I stand up to scan the crowd. But as I expected, I don't see giant poisonous snakes or jet packs anywhere.

"Everyone please join us for the Silly Clothes Race," announces Principal Klein, his loud voice cutting through the field.

The event is set up near the Hula-Hoop area. But I don't follow the crowd to the event. Instead, I stand and watch, looking for something that's out of place. Seth and Brian have already vanished from where they sat. I regret not watching them more closely. If anyone has put giant snakes inside clothes, it would be them.

Instead of going directly to the Silly Clothes Race, I make a beeline to where they sat. At first, I see nothing, but then I spot a small empty wrapper lying on the ground. I bend down to take a closer look.

It reads UNCLE SCRATCHY'S ITCHING POWDER. MADE FROM ACTUAL ROSE HIPS.

Itching powder. My fingers start to tingle just from touching the wrapper. I have no idea where anyone gets itching powder, but if anyone would know, it would be Brian and Seth.

I quicken my pace to the event.

By the time I arrive, Principal Klein is already talking to the contestants, explaining the rules. Two boxes of clothes sit by the starting line; one box is colored red and one is blue. Odd clothes overflow from the boxes: giant clown shoes, a business suit, a top hat, boas, and more. I don't see any suits of armor, so that's one less thing to worry about.

I spy Brian standing with Seth on the sidelines, snickering. Then I see Simon.

Brian's brother walks briskly toward the boxes of clothes. Since everyone watches Principal Klein and the contestants, no one notices Simon sneaking around, holding a small jar filled with red powder.

It doesn't take a genius to know what's in that jar. As soon as the first Team Red competitor puts on clothes, he or she will be too busy scratching to run.

I cut through the crowd, elbowing past Kyle. "Watch where you're going. Maybe try slowing?" he says, annoyed.

But I'm already past him, ducking around Gavin and Cooper on my way to those silly clothes boxes.

Simon stands next to them, untwisting the cap of his jar.

I break free of the pack, almost colliding into Trevor. "Be careful, you idiot!" shouts Trevor, angrily.

Mr. Foley frowns and turns to Adam, who stands near Trevor. "Watch your language or you'll be sent to the principal's office."

"But I didn't say anything," complains Adam. "It was Trevor."

"No excuses, young man," says a stern Mr. Foley.

I hear Adam spends a lot of time in the principal's office for all sorts of things.

Mr. Foley isn't watching me, and neither is anyone else as I near Simon, who is now tipping the jar over the Team Red box. The first few grains of powder float down, but a slight breeze blows them away, past the clothes and onto the grass.

Simon crouches down, closer to the box.

I hope a tornado might swoop in and blow away the itching powder, but I don't see any tornados. I also don't see the table in front of me.

I smack into it with my leg. The table, which is an unsteady folding table, wobbles. The portable fan that rests on top of it skids and falls off the table.

I grab the fan to keep it from crashing onto the ground. I catch the base, careful not to grab hold of the guard, the part that houses the whirling blade. But I accidentally hit the switch from medium to high.

The fan is powerful and pointing directly at Simon.

WHOOSH!

The itching powder sprinkles out the jar and immediately blows back into Simon, covering his shirt and his face. He's coated in red powder.

Simon's face changes from a mischievous sneer to a horrified grimace. He drops the jar to the ground. He madly scratches his cheeks and chest. "Help! Help!"

Everyone turns to look at him as he itches and jumps around and screams, "Water! I need water!" I return the fan gently atop the table and step slowly back.

Simon is now spinning in crazy circles before finally sprinting off, toward the supply shed and the sprinklers.

As he dashes farther and farther away, the crowd seems to lose interest. Meanwhile, Simon keeps yelling, "Water! Water!" and furiously scratching himself.

"He must be very thirsty," says Mr. Foley.

"Well, it is hot out here." Principal Klein turns to the contestants and claps his hands. "Anyway, let's get dressed," he announces to the racers.

I spot Brian and Seth. Their grins are gone as they watch Simon dashing away.

Meanwhile, the racers take their positions. The first racer will dress at the starting line before dashing to the next racer. Eric is running first for my team, and Tara starts for Team Red. According to Eric's text, he can change out of his clothes in sixteen seconds, which is pretty amazing, I think. He and Tara each slip on fuzzy vests, two weird hats, giant shoes, two business suits, a couple of purple boas, and mittens.

The racers will be hot, but silly.

But at least whoever wins this race will win fairly.

44
LILLY

I exchange high fives with just about everyone on my team, and now my palm hurts after so many slaps. When we won the Silly Clothes Race, our entire team, including me, went crazy with jumping and hollering and celebrating. Even Charlie jumped up and down, although I think he forgot about his broken foot, because after one hop he fell over and knocked down two other kids.

Our win also means we're in the lead again for the week. We're that much closer to winning our own island, or whatever secret prize we get. Zachary says we all get an island, and the island is made of cotton candy, but I think he's just making that up.

I had a lot to do with our winning, too. Instead of just picking kids to compete alphabetically, I spent a few minutes thinking about the event. Fast dressing was important, so I picked kids who like to wear strange clothes to school, like

Koko, who always seems layered in four shirts, and Zane, who wears weird sweaters with many zippers.

I knew they had lots of practice changing and unchanging and zipping and unzipping.

I'll need to be just as clever when choosing the rest of my teams today.

The other kids on Team Red noticed, too. Finn actually smiled at me and said, "Good job, Captain," and while Sarah didn't exactly smile at me (I don't think she can smile in any way other than evilly), she didn't glare, either.

Maybe my team doesn't think I'm working against them anymore, but I am still working against their cheating. I promised George and myself we would play fair, and those are two people I will never break a promise to again.

The next event is Flag Football. Football is a tough sport, so I've chosen kids who seem tough, like Finn and Sarah. They were easy choices.

I'm going to play, even though I'm not that tough, but I can be tough when I need to be. I've never played football, but it seems pretty easy. Someone throws the ball, and you catch it, and you keep on running until someone from the other team grabs your flag.

I join my team on the sidelines. Finn slaps me on the back. "Don't worry. Team Blue won't be able to stop us."

"No they won't," agrees Sarah, grinning. She holds our bag of flags and hands a flag to each of us. The flags are long red ribbons attached to a belt with Velcro, so the other team can easily rip them off. Each belt has two ribbons attached to it.

I buckle my belt around my waist while Sarah continues passing out the rest of the belts. I tug on my flag because I want to see how easily it rips off.

My flag doesn't budge.

I tug on it again, and again it doesn't move, like it's stuck. Then I see Sarah handing a belt to Norm, and pulling out a giant stapler.

That's when I notice that my flags are attached to my belt with about a dozen staples.

"What are you doing?" I ask Sarah, demanding an answer as she hands a stapled belt to Finn.

"What needs to be done," she says with a smirk.

"Both teams come here to begin, please," announces Principal Klein. He waits in the middle of the field.

Sarah tosses the bag and the stapler to the sidelines, and jogs toward our principal.

"I told you to stop it!" I shout. "Come back here!"

"Too late now," Sarah calls over her shoulder as she races away from me.

I join the other football players as our principal asks, "Are you ready to have fun?"

Sarah smirks, and so do other members of my team. I watch the faces of the players on Team Blue and many of them seem to smirk, too. But I don't think they would be smirking if they knew our scheme.

A guilty lump builds in my throat and I can't cough it up.

"General football rules apply," instructs Principal Klein. "To advance the ball you must pass it to another player. If you have the ball and someone removes your flag, the play is down at that spot. Team Red will have the ball first. We'll play for fifteen minutes. Whoever scores the most touchdowns wins."

As my team jogs to the other end of the field, Zachary laughs and tugs one of his unmovable flags. Sarah laughs, too, but I'm so upset that I can't keep my hands from shaking. There's nothing I can do without admitting we're cheaters, and then the entire day will be canceled and we'll all be in deep trouble.

Principal Klein blows his whistle, and Zachary hikes the ball to Finn, who shovels a quick pass back to Zachary. Danny from Team Blue swipes at Zachary's flag. But the flag doesn't budge.

"What's going on?" yells Danny, but Zachary is already racing away from him. Lacey, Pedro, and Kim from Team Blue all converge on Zachary. They surround him, each yanking on Zachary's flag, but it still doesn't move.

"What's going on?" they all cry out.

Zachary is all by himself now, sprinting down the field and easily scoring a touchdown. He spikes the football on the ground and shakes his legs in some sort of weird touchdown celebration. He looks like a wobbly legged flamingo, bobbing his head and zigzagging his skinny legs.

The rest of my team runs down the field to congratulate him, except me.

This is not something worth jumping up and down about, or feeling good about. We scored because we cheated.

Now it's Team Blue's turn with the ball. Cooper hikes the ball to Gavin, who tosses it to Danny. Danny bursts through the line and veers to his left, right at me. I'm ready. I stand my ground and swipe my hand to his belt and grip the flag.

I yank as hard as I can, but the flag doesn't move.

Now it's my turn to yell, "What's going on?"

As Danny runs down the field for an easy score, I find myself standing near the Team Blue sidelines. George calls out to me loudly, but not so loudly that teachers or our principal can hear, "Someone superglued our flags!"

The game continues. We hike the ball and score a touchdown, even though five or six kids grab at our flags. Team Blue hikes the ball and scores a touchdown, despite five or six of my teammates grabbing at the flags.

"What great running!" exclaims Principal Klein. The game is not very long, but I'm betting it's tied at about a zillion to a zillion. Principal Klein says, "You guys are all really good. I've never seen such a great game." I simply nod and force a fake smile. "But we only have time for one last play."

Since Danny on Team Blue has just scored his sixteenth touchdown, we have the ball.

There's only way to keep us from winning. If we don't score, the game will end in a tie. But it won't be easy to stop my team from scoring, unless I stop us myself.

As we huddle for our next play I bark, "Throw me the ball."

Finn eyes me. Sarah frowns. My entire team looks at me. They don't trust me. "Will you catch it?" Finn asks.

I nod.

"Will you score?" he asks.

"Just throw me the ball," I order. I'm our team captain, after all.

We walk to the line. My plan is simple: I'll catch the ball, run a few feet, and then drop the ball. The ball will roll out of bounds, and the game will end in a tie.

"Hike!" yells Finn.

Zachary hikes the ball to Finn, who then tosses it to me. I'm only about two feet away so it's an easy catch. Then I run toward the line where the entire Team Blue is waiting for me.

I run straight into them. I know they can't stop me. But I can stop myself.

Kyle grabs one of my flags. Daisy grabs another. I feel a dozen hands grabbing at my belt.

And then I trip, and I don't even trip over someone's foot but my own foot as I move to my right. As I fall, the ball squirts out of my hands, and not even on purpose.

The ball bounces on the ground once, twice, and then it takes a surprisingly large hop and lands right in Zachary's grasp.

Zachary runs forward, zipping past the outstretched arms of Team Blue as they reach for his flag, but they have no chance of ripping it free. Zachary runs across the open field.

Soon, he's performing his tenth silly touchdown dance of the day, his legs gyrating as if on swivels.

Principal Klein blows his whistle. "What a great game! Team Red wins!"

On the sidelines my teammates jump and whoop. They all pile on top of Zachary in the end zone, celebrating like we just won the Super Bowl.

I watch the fun. Our team has the lead, and I feel simply terrible about it.

45

GEORGE

Lilly and I run ahead of the pack so we can check out the next event: the Blind Potato Race. Large Idaho potatoes lie spread across a field. One person on each team wears a blindfold while picking up as many potatoes as she or he can. The rest of the team shouts directions such as, "Turn right! Bend down!"

But Lilly heard from Aisha, who heard from Taylor, who heard from Brianna, that Grace made slight alterations to the blindfolds. I remove one from the Team Red box, which sits on the folding table near the event. Running my finger along it, I immediately detect a small slit. That rip would have been impossible for Principal Klein to notice, but if you wrap the blindfold around your eyes, you can see right through it.

Lilly finds an extra blindfold in the Team Blue box, so I put the sabotaged blindfold in my back pocket and replace it with the new, unripped one, just as the rest of the class converges on the area.

I feel good that no one is cheating, but once the contest begins I don't feel so good about the team I picked.

Ten people are on each team, and it is clear my team is in trouble.

I picked players I thought might give good directions, but there are way too many directions.

"Go right!" yells Maggie.

"No, left!" yells Paige.

"No, right and then left!" yells Lacey.

"Do all of those," says Mario.

"No, no, no!" whines Maggie.

Blindfolded Eric keeps spinning randomly, bending down to almost pick up a potato, and then veering off to almost pick up another potato. When time expires, he has only grabbed two spuds, and he only nabbed those because he stepped on them. Meanwhile, Team Red picked up more than a dozen potatoes. I'm disappointed we didn't do better, but at least no one cheated.

I just wish Zachary wouldn't do his weird zigzagging victory dance every time Team Red wins something, though. It's annoying.

Our team is now down a whole bunch of points, too. I do the math in my head. We have to win the rest of today's events, or Team Red will be crowned Spirit Week champion.

Winning fairly is more important than winning, so at least

we'll lose fairly, sort of. But I guess I want to win a little more than I thought I did. I've never thought much about winning things before, but as our team captain, it's my responsibility to help us win. Even if I still really don't want to be our team captain.

Seth and Brian frown at me. All my planning hasn't done us much good. I spent a lot of time picking team members for the events, and we're way behind.

But we still have a chance.

The next event is the Rubber Chicken Throw, where kids take turns throwing a rubber chicken as far as they can. While Principal Klein explains the rules, George and I inspect the chickens. Sure enough, George spots foul play. Or, as he whispers while holding the chicken, *"Fowl* play." The Team Blue chicken is a lot heavier than ours, which would make it hard for them to throw. George shakes the chicken upside down and a few dozen marbles pour out of its mouth. He cuffs them in his hands and dumps them under a nearby table.

Soon, the event begins, and Ryan from Team Blue is up first. I hear she's the best pitcher on a travel softball team, and while chickens aren't softballs, I figure she might be really good. She grabs a chicken in her hand and starts twirling. I always see her twirling at school, but now she twirls faster and faster, and I hope that maybe it will make her too dizzy to throw straight. But her twirls seem to propel her arm forward, and the chicken soars out of her hand.

Chickens, however, are not softballs. Her chicken flops only fifteen feet away.

I smile, although not too much, because smiling when someone else does poorly isn't nice. But it turns out that no one can throw the chicken very far. It seems that rubber chickens don't fly well, but after a few tosses we have the lead, which is awesomesauce. I think Team Blue is finished, because all we have to do is win one more event and we will win Spirit Week, but then Brian from Team Blue steps up and hurls his chicken ten feet farther than anyone else.

He unleashes a wild yowl of excitement when his team is awarded the victory.

While Brian is being congratulated for his rubber chicken toss, George and I don't waste time watching. We need to hurry to the next event, the Water Balloon Toss.

But when we get to the water balloon station, we find a whole bunch of marbles on the ground and no balloons in sight.

Soon, Principal Klein is talking with one of the parent volunteers. He frowns, nods, frowns, nods, and then finally explains to everyone that they found holes in all of the balloons so the event has been changed. "Faulty balloons. It happens," he says, but I'm pretty sure I know who's at fault.

Sarah and Grace look at each other and frown. Brian and Seth look at each and frown, too. I can only guess that they all had the same idea, but at least they can't sabotage a brand-new competition.

Our principal explains that the event has been changed to Marble Toes, and kids need to pick up as many marbles as they can using only their toes and then drop them into either a red bucket or a blue bucket.

But I can see we're in trouble just by looking at everyone's feet. Team Blue has a whole bunch of players with big feet, like Jamaal. His feet look gigantic and after the event starts he picks up three times more marbles than anyone else.

Sure enough, when Mrs. Rosenbloom blows her whistle to end the game, it's not even close. Team Blue has more than twice as many marbles in their bucket as we do.

We still have a small lead, but Tug-of-War, the final event of the day, is worth double points.

So whoever wins Tug-of-War wins Spirit Week.

47

GEORGE

Both teams gather around Principal Klein, and a rope lies on the ground next to his feet. Our principal clears his throat. "It's been a wonderful day, hasn't it?"

Most of us clap and cheer, but I just let out a sigh. I want the day to be done. It's exhausting uncovering secret plots. Our principal wipes his brow. "Even though it's so very, very hot."

Lilly and I look at each other. I can't read minds, but I can read her mind because she's thinking the same thing as me: *Please, please, please let us just get through this last event without any tricks.*

"You have all displayed great sportsmanship today," says Principal Klein. "I knew you had it in you."

I bite my lip.

"We had some, um, difficulties in the beginning of the day, but that was no fault of yours," Principal Klein continues. I'm standing right next to our principal, and he pats me on the head. "If each captain will send twelve members of their team for our final contest, we'll begin. Whoever wins the Tug-of-War wins the entire Spirit Week. How exciting."

I jog back to my team.

I feel good about our chances. With Brian, Seth, and Kyle all on my team, I don't see how we can lose.

But then I look around. Where are Brian and Seth?

48
LILLY

My team huddles around me, and suddenly I'm bombarded by a flurry of sneers and plotting.

"We need to win, and win that prize," says Grace. "No matter what."

"No matter what," Sarah agrees.

"I love prizes," says Amelia.

"I just love winning," says Sarah.

"Oh, we'll win," says Grace. She chuckles. It's a mean-sounding chuckle.

"Guys, let's just win fairly," I plead. "Please."

That magic word works with adults, but it doesn't always work with kids, unfortunately.

"Do you have the grease?" Grace asks Finn.

Finn nods and removes a tube of some sort of lubricant from his pocket. "We just need to smear it on the Team Blue side of the rope. The rope will slide off their hands. They won't be able to tug at all."

"We'll need to distract everyone while you rub it on," says Sarah. "I'll pretend I see a snake or something and start screaming."

"I don't like snakes," says Grace.

I puff out my chest and walk right into the middle of their small conspiracy circle. Enough is enough, and I've had enough of all of them. "We need to win this event fairly. Stop ruining everything. Let the best team win."

"Everyone knows that winning is everything," says Sarah. "And losing is for losers."

"No, cheating is for losers," I say. "And that's what you and Grace are, and you too, Finn. A bunch of cheating losers."

"But what about the prize?" says Amelia, who stands just outside our circle.

"I'm with Lilly," says Aisha. She shoves past a couple of smaller kids and puts her arm around my shoulders. "We're not cheating."

"I agree," says Colby, and she puts her arms around Aisha's shoulders. "We need to win fairly. That's what we do in golf."

"Me too," says Alex. "I mean, I think we should win fairly. I don't play golf."

"Me three," says Liam. "About the winning fairly part."

We are joined together, our hands on our shoulders, a line of Team Red players vowing to play without cheating. More teammates join us, and soon more than half the team is lined up, all staring at Sarah, Grace, and Finn.

"I just wanted a horseback ride," Finn says in a soft voice and taking a small step back.

"Forget you guys," says Sarah. "I'll spread the grease." She holds her hand out to Finn, demanding he hand over the tube, which he does.

I shake my head. "No way."

"Teams take your positions," orders our principal from the Tug-of-War rope.

Finn, Grace, and Sarah step forward. They were all chosen to participate. But I break our arms-on-shoulders Team Red line and step in front of them. "You guys are sitting this one out."

"What are you talking about?" asks Sarah.

"Sit down," I demand. "All of you."

"I'm the strongest person on the team," argues Finn.

"Maybe," I say. "But you three have been nothing but cheaters from the beginning. I'd rather lose by playing fair than win by playing with cheaters." I turn to the rest of the team. "Noah, Aisha, and Tara—take their places."

"Are you kidding?" demands Sarah. "Do you want to lose?"

"I want to play fair." I turn my back to her.

"Then you're a loser," barks Grace. She stares at me, her stares carving little notches of hate into me.

But I don't care. I'm team captain. I might not be the most organized team captain ever, but I'm an honest one.

I hope I'm a winning one, too.

49

GEORGE

After I call out the names to compete in Tug-of-War, my stomach sinks. I see Brian and Seth. They are standing near the back of our group, with Simon. I twist my mouth into a frown. They're huddling and laughing. They must be plotting.

This ends now.

"Hey, where are you going?" asks Luke as I march past him. "We need to get everyone on the field!"

I keep going.

"Do you have the egg salad?" Brian asks Simon.

Simon nods. He holds a bucket. "Still had some left from the other day."

Seth cringes. "That egg salad smells worse than wet dog fur."

Simon nods. "Egg salad doesn't stay fresh very long. It's turning a little green, too."

I barge into their group. "Stop it!"

Simon looks at me, and frowns. "You again?" He shakes his head. "Just go away, okay? We're going to win this event. Without your help."

"You guys are going to stop this right now." They glare at me, and their shadows loom over me. I feel very, very small.

They turn their backs to me. Simon barks orders to Brian and Seth. "You guys dump the egg salad on the ground near Team Red. They'll be too busy slipping and sliding to pull their rope." He hands the bucket to his brother.

"Stop!" I shout, as loudly as I can. The three conspirators turn around while I ball my hands into fists and take a deep breath. "You guys are not doing anything anymore. You've helped ruin this entire week with all your plotting. You know, I thought winning was about note taking and organization. But Lilly was right. Spirit Week is about spirit. And you guys have no spirit, and no place on this team. Not anymore. I'm done keeping quiet. This ends now."

I grab the bucket handle, still in Brian's grip.

"Let go!" He yanks his hand away, but I keep my grip tight. He pulls his hand, and I pull toward me, as if we're starting our own game of bucket Tug-of-War. I yank as hard as I can, and the bucket falls from his grip. I drop it, too. The egg salad splatters to the ground next to us.

"Look what you've done," Brian complains.

"Teams take your positions," orders our principal.

Simon steps forward, his eyes fixed on me. "If we lose today it's all because of . . ." He never finishes his sentence. He steps into the egg salad, and as promised, it's slippery. His legs slide. He skids. He reaches out to Brian to keep his balance, but all he does is make Brian teeter, too. Brian's legs hit Seth, who topples over and smashes into Brian.

A moment later they are all on the ground and covered in old, smelly, and slightly green egg salad.

I turn my back to them and pick two new Team Blue players to take their places. I know we'll probably lose now, but I still can't wipe a great big smile from my face.

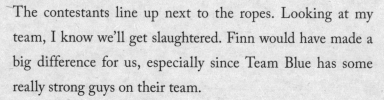

50

LILLY

The contestants line up next to the ropes. Looking at my team, I know we'll get slaughtered. Finn would have made a big difference for us, especially since Team Blue has some really strong guys on their team.

But when I look at the field, I notice Seth and Brian, who are the biggest Team Blue kids, aren't on the field, either. They stand on the sidelines frowning, arms crossed, and covered in some disgusting-looking yellowish-green stuff, glaring at George.

"Grab your ropes!" shouts Principal Klein.

The teams do.

"On the count of three!" announces Principal Klein.

George smiles at me from across the field. I smile back.

"One . . . ," begins Principal Klein.

"When we lose, it will be all your fault," Grace barks from next to me on the sidelines.

"Two . . . ," continues our principal.

"If the prize is a million dollars, I'll never talk to you again," threatens Sarah.

"Three!" yells Principal Klein.

The teams tug.

The rope inches toward the Team Blue side almost immediately, and I fear the worst. But then our team pulls harder and it inches back to our side.

"Go, Team Red!" I shout. My teammates repeat my cry. "Go, Team Red! Go, Team Red!"

"Go, Team Blue!" shouts the other side. "Go, Team Blue!"

The rope inches one way, and then the other, back and forth and back. The two teams appear to be evenly matched.

"Come on, guys!" I holler.

"Pull for one million dollars!" shouts Amelia. "Or something just as great!"

"Pull! Pull!" I shout, clapping and yelling encouragement. As our team captain, I will urge my team to victory with spirit and fairness.

Both teams tug, the rope inching first one way and then the other.

"C'mon, guys!" I hear George yell from the other side.

"Go, Team Blue!" roars his team behind him.

"Go, Team Red!" I shout, followed by the rest of my team.

The rope moves to our side by a foot, and then two feet to the other.

Kyle, who pulls for Team Blue, grunts loudly. Aisha on my team grunts even louder.

I feel a tap on my shoulder. When I turn, Sarah glowers at me. "You are never sleeping over at my house, you know. Or having lunch with us ever again."

I shrug. "Good. I'd rather eat with George anyway."

"Losers eating together," snarls Sarah.

"I guess that's why you and Grace always eat alone," I answer. I turn my back to her with a smirk just in time to see both teams collapse in a giant heap.

Behind me, I hear our principal cry out. "Team Blue wins!"

51
GEORGE

Everyone on my team meets in the middle of the field, jumping up and down and hugging. A few of us scream. Eric gives me a big squeeze, and so do Luke and Kyle. Kyle squeezes a little too hard, and my bones ache.

Even Brian throws me a thumbs-up. If there are sore feelings lingering from my removing him from the Tug-of-War competition, he doesn't show it. Winning makes everyone happy.

"Do you think we'll get our big-screen televisions immediately?" asks Toby.

"Or maybe we all win saxophones," Luke suggests, fidgeting and clapping.

Now I can see why Lilly is always so competitive. I don't think there is a much greater feeling in the world than winning something, especially when you earn that win with hard work and fair play.

But there is one problem with winning. It means someone else lost. Team Red stands on the sidelines watching us, their faces fixed with sad frowns. I see a tear or two.

But the person who makes me feel worst about winning is Lilly. Her shoulders slump. She stands alone, no one else on the team near her. She's like an island of unhappiness.

Winning isn't worth winning if it means your best friend loses. My victory feels hollow. As my team continues to jump and scream, I trudge across the field to Lilly. She looks up at me, her eyes watery. "Sorry we won," I say.

"Never be sorry for winning. Enjoy it. I'm happy for you."

"You don't look happy."

"I can be sad for me and happy for you at the same time. Now get back there with your team and celebrate."

I want to give her a hug and apologize, but I have nothing to apologize for. I take her advice and rejoin my team. As soon as I enter our circle of joy, I get slapped on the back and congratulated by almost everyone.

"The best team captain ever," exclaims Danny.

"You're not so bad, I guess," says Seth.

Principal Klein walks forward. We all quiet down, controlling our celebration as he clears his throat.

"Team Blue, you won with good sportsmanship and teamwork. I'm proud of each and every one of you today."

I glance at the sidelines. Lilly cracks a grin through her

gloom. If Principal Klein knew the truth about today, I don't think he would be quite so proud.

"As promised, Team Blue will win a special prize." We hold our breath. This is the moment we've worked all week to reach.

"I bet it's our own penguin," says Gavin.

"Or maybe fashion accessories for a year," suggests Samantha.

"Or someone will write a book about us," says Adam, but we all shake our heads because that idea is ridiculous.

"But because you played so fairly today, the prize will go to the entire fifth grade," our principal announces.

Our entire side goes quiet, and our excitement sort of leaks out. No one says a word, until finally Brian yells out, "That's not fair!"

Principal Klein ignores the shout. "Next week, the fifth-grade class will go on a field trip—an exciting field trip. One that I'm sure all of you will love."

I lean in, as does the rest of my team.

"I bet we're going to our own private island," says Luke.

"Sweden!" guesses Bjorn.

"It's a trip to the new science center downtown," announces Principal Klein, raising his large hands in triumph and throwing us all a giant smile. "Isn't that great?"

Maggie yells out, "I knew it! Wow!" But the rest of the grade isn't sure if we should celebrate or frown. A few of us clap. A field trip is better than nothing, but we were all imagining grander things.

"No penguins?" burbles Gavin.

"I hear the science center is terrific," exclaims Principal Klein. We clap, but Lacey, Paige, and Maggie clap loudest and longest.

Principal Klein looks around, puzzled, as he finally seems to realize his announcement hasn't generated the excitement he thought it might. "I think you'll all find it's wonderfully educational." Our principal clears his throat. "But don't forget you will all still need to help with Ms. Bryce's after-school tutoring club, too." This generates even more enthusiastic clapping from Maggie and her friends. I think her arm cast makes her claps louder, although I'm surprised it isn't painful for her.

Our principal continues. "I truly hope this newfound teamwork continues as you finish the year and move on to middle school next year. Now, everyone head to the cafeteria for the special end-of-Spirit-Week dessert."

That gets a shout of enthusiasm from the crowd. Who doesn't like dessert? Our principal marches toward school, and we all follow him like a flock of hungry sheep.

Lilly catches up to me. She reaches out and holds my hand. She gives it a squeeze. "I can't believe we all won that prize. I bet that was the plan all along."

I nod. "Probably. It's the sort of thing adults do."

"At least we get to eat," says Cooper, jogging near us. "It's a Field Day tradition to eat snickerdoodle brownies from the Fireside Bakery. Those are my favorites."

The Fireside Bakery is sort of famous for their snickerdoodle brownies.

The first thing I'm going to do is wash my hands, though. I'm still annoyed I ran out of hand sanitizer. I can't pick up a brownie with such grubby fingers.

I file into the cafeteria along with the rest of my class. But as we enter, a gasp resounds across the room. The cafeteria reeks of eggs.

"I know you'll enjoy this special dessert," says Principal Klein. "Egg salad!"

Lilly practically collapses by my side in disappointment. Everyone was excited for brownies, but that excitement spills out of us like a bucket of water with a hole in it.

"This has to be the worst Field Day victory ever," Luke mumbles, who is so disappointed he's not even wiggling.

As we stare at one another, horrified, a loud laugh booms across the room. Principal Klein slaps his knee. "Oh, I'm just kidding." He shrugs. "It was left over from the faculty lunch today. I'm not sure why everyone doesn't love egg salad as much as I do."

Teachers and parent volunteers stream from the cafeteria doors. They each wheel a cart of snickerdoodle brownies.

Everyone cheers, and then rushes toward the desserts.

I'm near the back, but there's a bunch of commotion and shoving as students elbow one another to reach the carts. I hear Mr. Foley say, "Knock it off, Brian. And you only get one brownie."

After a few minutes, when my hands are washed, we all have our treats, and I'm happily munching on the best brownie on the planet, I sit at my usual cafeteria table with Lilly. We exchange grins. "Too bad we don't have Spirit Week next year," she says. "We'd beat you guys if we had another try." Her smile turns to a frown. "And we'd win at any cost."

I choke on my brownie, but Lilly starts giggling and I know she's only joking.

"If there's a next time, we'll be on the same team," I say.

Lilly squeezes my arm. "Of course. It's only worth winning if you win with the people you care about the most."

I squeeze her arm back. As I take another bite of brownie, I glance at my friendship bracelet. Spirit Week wasn't exactly what I thought it would be, and I'm glad we don't have to go through it again. But the science center will be fun, especially since I'll be going with Lilly.

She looks up at me, bouncing on her seat and with brownie crumbs on her lips. "And George, next time we play tic-tac-toe, don't let me win, okay?"

"Let you win? I would never . . ."

Lilly shakes her head. "No one loses two hundred and twenty-eight times in a row in tic-tac-toe unless they are trying to lose, George. I mean, I think that's sort of impossible."

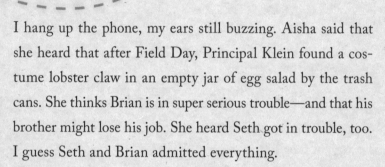

52
LILLY

I hang up the phone, my ears still buzzing. Aisha said that she heard that after Field Day, Principal Klein found a costume lobster claw in an empty jar of egg salad by the trash cans. She thinks Brian is in super serious trouble—and that his brother might lose his job. She heard Seth got in trouble, too. I guess Seth and Brian admitted everything.

Grace and Sarah didn't get into trouble, but no one would talk to them after Field Day. I don't think anyone likes them much anymore. Finn was especially angry when he heard that Grace doesn't own a horse.

I'm just glad the week is over and I can relax. I lie on my bed, looking first at my clay figurines, and then at my bulletin board, the one filled with pictures of George and me. I'm glad I didn't rip them up the other day. I love looking at them. It seems every time I've had fun, it's been with George.

"Lilly, it's time to go out to eat!" Mom yells up from downstairs.

I almost forgot that it's Friday night, restaurant night, and we're going to a new Mexican restaurant. It was George's idea. He usually lets me pick where we eat, but I insisted that he should choose this time.

I jump off the bed. I put on a clean shirt—I'm still wearing my Team Red shirt from school and it sort of smells like eggs—and I think back on the week. Despite all the problems, I guess everything worked out. I mean, I couldn't ask for a better ending to the week than eating at a restaurant with my best friend.

Or, at least, I couldn't have asked for a better ending to the week that didn't include winning a million dollars or a free penguin. Great friends are much more important than that stuff, anyway.

ACKNOWLEDGMENTS

When I was a kid, if I had been a better athlete, or singer, or artist, I might not have been immediately drawn to writing, so I need to thank my parents for passing me their un-athletic, un-musical, and un-artistic genes. But they also passed on their love and encouragement, which is really all that matters, or at least mostly.

I also need to thank Lauren, Madelyn, and Emmy for putting up with me, because I'm sometimes grumpy or stressed and I work out of the house a lot. And although I work mostly secreted away in my home office, they still have to deal with that grumpiness and anxiousness more than they should, although they do it pretty well, all things considered, and don't make me feel bad about it, most of the time at least.

It goes without saying that I am extremely thankful to the entire Scholastic team, but I'll say it anyway—I am extremely thankful to the entire Scholastic team, and most especially my brilliant editor Jody Corbett who inspires, lifts up, and encourages me every step along the way, and as any writer knows, any book has a whole lot of steps to climb before you reach the end.

Also, thanks to Paper Dog Studio for the fun cover, Lissy Marlin for the awesome chapter illustrations, and to Yaffa Jaskoll for her book design. I am fortunate to have such talent around me.

Lastly, I want to thank the teachers at Districts 73 and 128, who have provided our family and our community with such a wonderful and rich educational experience.

ABOUT THE AUTHOR

Allan Woodrow participated in his school's fifth-grade Field Day many years ago. He was leading the Fast Walking event until he was disqualified for running and not walking. Allan is still bitter about this.

When he wasn't losing Field Day events, Allan was writing. Since then, he has gone on to write the novels *Class Dismissed* (a companion to *Unschooled*) and *The Pet War*, as well as other books for young readers, written under secret names. His writing also appears in the Scholastic anthology *Lucky Dog: Twelve Tales of Rescued Dogs*.

Allan currently lives near Chicago. He regularly visits schools and libraries, and sometimes is even invited to speak in them. For more about Allan and his books, visit his website at www.allanwoodrow.com.

CLASS 507 IS TEACHER-FREE!

CLASS DISMISSED

ALLAN WOODROW

21 students - 1 teacher + 1 ginormous secret =
9,372 THINGS THAT CAN GO ABSOLUTELY, COMPLETELY, HORRIBLE WRONG